FROM THE
NANCY DREW FILES

THE CASE: Nancy tries to track down a hospital killer—and prove a young doctor's innocence.

CONTACT: Ned's friend Trevor Callahan is blamed for the death of a special patient—his fiancée's father.

SUSPECTS: April Shaw—the beautiful med student is her father's sole heir.

David Baines—the hospital orderly loves luxury— and knows where the bodies are buried.

Trevor Callahan—the young M.D. seems prone to making lethal mistakes.

COMPLICATIONS: The only thing that can clear Trevor is an autopsy on Dr. Shaw—but April's father has suddenly vanished!

Books in The Nancy Drew Files® Series

#1	SECRETS CAN KILL	#19	SISTERS IN CRIME
#2	DEADLY INTENT	#20	VERY DEADLY YOURS
#3	MURDER ON ICE		
#4	SMILE AND SAY MURDER	#21	RECIPE FOR MURDER
#5	HIT AND RUN HOLIDAY	#22	FATAL ATTRACTION
		#23	SINISTER PARADISE
#6	WHITE WATER TERROR	#24	TILL DEATH DO US PART
#7	DEADLY DOUBLES		
#8	TWO POINTS TO MURDER	#25	RICH AND DANGEROUS
#9	FALSE MOVES	#26	PLAYING WITH FIRE
#10	BURIED SECRETS	#27	MOST LIKELY TO DIE
#11	HEART OF DANGER	#28	THE BLACK WIDOW
#12	FATAL RANSOM	#29	PURE POISON
#13	WINGS OF FEAR	#30	DEATH BY DESIGN
#14	THIS SIDE OF EVIL	#31	TROUBLE IN TAHITI
#15	TRIAL BY FIRE	#32	HIGH MARKS FOR MALICE
#16	NEVER SAY DIE		
#17	STAY TUNED FOR DANGER	#33	DANGER IN DISGUISE
		#34	VANISHING ACT
#18	CIRCLE OF EVIL	#35	BAD MEDICINE

Available from ARCHWAY paperbacks

THE NANCY DREW FILES
CASE · 35

BAD MEDICINE

Carolyn Keene

AN ARCHWAY PAPERBACK
Published by POCKET BOOKS
New York   London   Toronto   Sydney   Tokyo

AN ARCHWAY PAPERBACK *Original*

An Archway Paperback published by
POCKET BOOKS, a division of Simon & Schuster Inc.
1230 Avenue of the Americas, New York, NY 10020

ISBN: 0-671-64702-4

First Archway Paperback printing May 1989

10 9 8 7 6 5 4 3 2 1

NANCY DREW, AN ARCHWAY PAPERBACK and colophon are registered trademarks of Simon & Schuster Inc.

THE NANCY DREW FILES is a trademark of Simon & Schuster Inc.

Printed in the U.S.A.

IL 7+

BAD
MEDICINE

Chapter

One

THE MAD DOCTOR bent over the young reddish-blond-haired girl strapped to his table. His scalpel glinted dangerously in the harsh glow from the overhead lights in the operating room. "You'll bother me no more!" he said with an evil cackle.

He lifted his hand high above her chest, ready to plunge the knife in.

Bess Marvin covered her eyes. "I can't look! Tell me when it's over!"

Nancy Drew glanced up from the television screen, amused by her friend's terrified look.

1

"Don't worry. The hero's about to come and save her."

"How can you tell?"

"By the music, Bess. It's definitely hero music," Nancy answered.

"Why can't she save herself?" asked George Fayne, Bess's cousin and one of Nancy's best friends.

"Because she's trapped with a maniac!" declared Bess, flipping her blond hair behind her ears.

At that moment the movie's hero threw open the door to the operating room and wrestled the doctor for the scalpel. The scalpel clattered to the floor, and the villainous doctor staggered toward the door. The heroine's eyes fluttered open.

"Oh, Robert . . ."

George jumped up from the couch and snapped the television set off, disgusted. "I can't stand a wimpy heroine."

"Me, neither." Nancy stretched and yawned. "I thought this movie would be better."

The three friends were seated in the Drews' den, eating popcorn and spending a quiet Saturday night at home.

"Since when are you interested in medical thrillers?" Bess asked as Nancy rewound the videotape.

"Since Ned decided to enroll in a week-long

seminar at Westmoor University Medical School," Nancy answered. Ned Nickerson was Nancy's steady boyfriend and a student at Emerson College. "All next week he'll be right here in River Heights, at the med school. He's going to be studying hospital administration."

"Hospital administration, huh?" George said. "Will he have any time off?"

"I don't know, but I hope so. I'm seeing him tomorrow night before the seminar starts, but I think he'll be pretty busy after that. His friend Trevor Callahan is a second-year resident at the school and hospital here, and I know Ned wants to spend time with him." Nancy hit the eject button, and the tape popped out of the machine.

"Trevor?" Bess asked. "I don't think I've met him."

"You haven't," Nancy admitted. "Actually, neither have I. Trevor's family has lived down the block from the Nickersons for a while, but Trevor's older than Ned and he's been off at medical school for years."

"He's a second-year resident? What exactly does that mean?" George asked, reaching for another handful of popcorn. "Is he still a student?"

"Well, yes—in a sense. But Trevor's a real doctor, too. He finished medical school, and now he's doing his residency."

"Well, Trevor won't take up all Ned's spare time, will he?" Bess asked. She pulled on her denim jacket. "You should still have some time for fun."

"I hope so."

Nancy walked Bess and George to the door, then locked up the house and climbed into bed, folding her arms under her head. She was eager for Sunday to come and for Ned to start his seminar.

"Trevor or no Trevor, you're going to spend some time with me, Ned Nickerson," Nancy said, staring up at the dark ceiling with a smile on her face.

"Are you sure you want to get involved in hospital administration?" Nancy asked Ned as she pulled against her seat belt to look out the windshield.

She was peering through the early-evening shadows, trying to get a good look at the prestigious medical school. The hospital, a huge gray stone building, stood in the forefront of the campus. A smaller building flanked it on the south. The dorms were clustered around the parking lot, and farther back, across a grassy parkway, stood an older ivy-covered brick building.

"Not exactly," Ned admitted, pulling into a parking spot near one of the dorms. It was four stories high, and a covered walkway extended from the front door to the parking lot. "That's why I'm attending this seminar—to see if I like the business end of running a hospital."

Nancy sent him a sidelong look. Ned was rugged and good-looking with an easy smile and an athletic build. She couldn't imagine anyone else being her steady boyfriend. She was thrilled to see him and spend time with him. "You know, I've always wondered what it would be like to work in a hospital."

Ned laughed. "Nurse Nancy, eh?" He tousled her reddish blond hair affectionately.

"Very funny. I was thinking more about *Doctor* Drew."

Grinning, Ned said, "Well, you're about to meet *Doctor* Callahan. Trevor said he and April, his fiancée, would meet us in front of this building. Then we're all going to dinner."

Nancy knew very little about Trevor except what Ned had told her. She knew he was specializing in cardiology, hoping to be a heart surgeon soon.

They waited in the car, but twenty minutes after they were supposed to meet, there was no sign of either Trevor or his fiancée. Eventually an attractive girl with blunt-cut shoulder-length brown hair pushed through the front doors of the dorm. She wore a blue dress, and what looked like a lab coat was tucked under one arm. She hesitated on the brightly lit stairs, peering through the covered walkway.

"Do you think that could be April?" Nancy asked.

"There's one way to find out." Ned climbed out of the car and called, "Are you April Shaw?"

"Yes," she answered. "Ned Nickerson?"

"The one and only."

April hurried toward Ned. "Trevor's going to be late. His shift was changed today, and he won't be off until after seven. I'm sorry. He tried to call but couldn't reach you."

Nancy opened her door and walked around the front of the car to meet April, who looked about twenty-three or -four. Though the evening was warm, her arms were wrapped around her waist, as if she felt cold. She kept glancing over her shoulder at the hospital building.

"This is my girlfriend, Nancy Drew," Ned said, introducing them.

Up close, Nancy could see that April had serious deep blue eyes and a small turned-up nose. "Hi," April said distractedly, shaking Nancy's hand. "I'm Dr. April Shaw."

"Doctor?" Nancy repeated, impressed.

April smiled faintly. "I'm in my third year of medical school. I won't be a full-fledged doctor until I'm finished, but we address one another as doctor as soon as we're admitted to medical school." She threw another look at the imposing gray building.

"Do you want to go to the hospital?" Nancy asked.

"Am I that obvious? Yes, I guess I do." She shook her head apologetically. "You see, Trevor's over there now checking on my father. He came to visit me last week, but three days ago he had a heart attack. Now he's a patient here, and I'm really worried about him."

"Oh, I'm sorry," Nancy murmured. Her heart went out to April.

They walked along a curving sidewalk to the hospital's main entrance. "My father is a doctor, too," April went on. She seemed anxious to air her problems. "Dr. Gerard Shaw. When I got accepted to med school here, he was the happiest man in the world. But then he got sick." She sighed heavily. "I didn't really want him to visit me. I was afraid the trip would be too much for him."

"You mean you thought he might have a heart attack?"

"He does have a heart condition," April admitted.

The hospital's main lobby was decorated in cool tones of gray and white. Several sofas were grouped around a rectangular glass table, and several magazines were fanned across the table's glossy surface. The reception hub took up the center of the room. Two women sat behind it, one greeting visitors and the other working the switchboard.

"Trevor's on seven—the cardiology floor," April explained as they stopped by the group of sofas. "He promised to check on my father. I won't bother him now; the doctors in CCU want him to rest."

"What's CCU?" Nancy asked.

"Cardiac Care Unit. The cardiac nurses staff it around the clock. I'm hoping my dad'll be well enough to be moved to a private room soon."

Nancy glanced at Ned. She didn't see how they could leave the hospital and go out to dinner. April was too upset. "Maybe we could eat in the hospital cafeteria," Nancy suggested out loud.

Ned grimaced. "Hospital food?" he repeated, clutching his throat as if he might gag. "How about going somewhere else? Anywhere else!"

"April might want to stay at the hospital," Nancy pointed out, nudging him in the ribs.

"No, that's okay," April insisted. "As soon as Trevor's through, I'd like to get away. I've been sick with worry all day." She looked at the clock on the far wall. "Do you mind waiting?"

"No problem," Nancy said, and they sat down in the lobby. Nancy started to ask April about being a doctor when a disembodied voice announced over the loudspeaker, "Dr. Trevor Callahan to Room seven fifty-five. Dr. Callahan. Room seven fifty-five. Stat."

"Now, what's that all about?" April muttered. "Nobody calls stat unless it's very serious. Come on," she added abruptly. "We'll meet Trevor on seven."

Nancy and Ned exchanged glances. They didn't want to get in the way of an emergency. But April had already ushered them to an elevator.

"The room's in the west wing," April said as they stepped off the elevator into a gleaming corridor.

A blond man in a doctor's coat was just pushing open the door to Room 755 when Nancy, Ned, and April approached. "There's Trevor now," April said, rushing forward.

Intent on his task, Trevor disappeared into the room. Nancy stood by the open door. Inside the room, someone was gasping wildly. Alarmed,

Nancy caught a clear glimpse of a middle-aged woman lying in bed, her face swollen and contorted, her fingers clutching at her throat.

"She's choking!" Nancy exclaimed.

But instead of helping her, Trevor just stood at the foot of the hospital bed, staring. Nancy was horrified. He was going to let her die!

Chapter

Two

Trevor SUDDENLY LEAPT FORWARD and pulled the woman's hands from her throat. Quick as a flash, he bent her head back to clear her air passage. "Get more help!" he yelled over his shoulder to the nurse who had run in. "I need an intubation! Something's wrong. Quick!"

"Penicillin," the patient wheezed out.

Nancy realized that Trevor had been hesitating because he was diagnosing what was wrong. Apparently this was serious.

The nurse turned on her heel, going for help. Before Nancy could move, she was nearly knocked over by a distinguished-looking doctor. "What's wrong?" he demanded tensely, rushing past her into the room.

"Dr. Callahan's ordered an intubation, Dr. Rayburn," the nurse called over her shoulder. She was already hurrying toward a hospital paging phone posted in the hallway.

"Call a code ninety-nine!" Trevor yelled after the nurse.

Rayburn took matters into his own hands. He snatched up the phone in the room. "Code ninety-nine, stat. This patient's suffering from penicillin poisoning!"

Nancy and Ned stepped away from the door of 755. "What's an intubation?" Ned asked Nancy. She shook her head.

When Nancy posed the same question to April, she said, "They're going to insert a tube into the patient's windpipe because she can't breathe on her own."

"Is that what code ninety-nine means?" Ned asked.

April looked grim. "No, that means cardiac arrest."

The hospital staff that had responded to the code finally began to disperse. Nancy, Ned, and April stayed back from the action, not wanting to get in the way. Finally only Trevor and Dr.

Rayburn remained inside the room. The patient's lungs were being artificially filled with oxygen. Nancy could see the little blips on the screen, which she assumed indicated the woman's heartbeat.

Trevor slowly walked out of the room. Now it was he who seemed to be in shock. The look he sent April was dazed and bleak. Dr. Rayburn shook his head and studied the patient's chart as he slowly walked out of the room. "Something's wrong," he said, as if to himself. "There's got to be a mistake here."

Trevor glanced over Dr. Rayburn's shoulder at the chart. The blood drained from his face and he turned chalky white.

"I don't know how this happened," Dr. Rayburn said seriously. "This patient should never have been given penicillin!"

Trevor nodded dumbly.

"Trevor, what's wrong?" April asked anxiously after Dr. Rayburn left.

"Nothing." He seemed to shake himself, focusing on Nancy and Ned for the first time. "I'm— uh—almost finished. I'll change and meet you out front in fifteen minutes."

"Are you all right?" April was obviously very worried.

"Yeah, I'm okay."

13

As they headed down the elevator, Ned whispered in Nancy's ear, "Now what was that all about?"

Nancy shook her head. She didn't know, but she'd gained the distinct impression that something was seriously wrong.

"How's Dad?" April asked Trevor as soon as the four of them were seated around a table at one of River Heights's most popular Mexican restaurants. A basket of corn chips sat in the center of the hand-painted blue- and gold-tiled tabletop.

Nancy studied Trevor for the first time. He was quite handsome, with blond hair and gray eyes that had sunbursts of laugh lines at the outer corners. Ned had assured her he was fun-loving and casual, yet he seemed so serious that Nancy couldn't imagine his having a sense of humor.

Trevor looked blankly at April for several seconds. "Oh, your father was okay when I checked in on him. The same as when you left."

"He's no better, then?"

Trevor moved his hand over to cover April's. "Give him time."

April looked so downcast that Nancy decided to try to change the subject. "How did you two meet?" she asked Trevor. "At medical school?"

He nodded. "April was in her first year and I

14

was in my fourth. I'd already decided to specialize in cardiology, so I'd geared my studies in that
direction. When April was assigned to Dr. Rayburn for cardiology we bumped into each other."

"Dr. Rayburn's a cardiologist?" Ned asked.

"The chief of cardiology," April corrected
him. "He's got quite a reputation at W.U."

"He's one of the main reasons I decided to take
my residency here at W.U. rather than apply to
another hospital," Trevor admitted.

Nancy smiled, glancing at April. "I can guess
the other reason."

Trevor smiled back, and Nancy caught her first
real glimpse of the man who was Ned's friend.
Once he was relaxed, Trevor wasn't so intimidat-
ing and serious. It was clear he adored April.

"How long is a residency?" Ned asked.

"Six years in cardiology," said Trevor.

"Wow. You'll be an old man before you finish!"

"I want to be the best cardiologist around.
That takes time. By the time April is through
with med school, we'll be ready to get married."

April and Trevor looked at each other and
smiled. Ned slipped his arm around Nancy's
shoulders. Nancy felt warm and happy. Someday
she'd like to make plans as April and Trevor
were. From the sweet glance Ned sent her, she
could tell he was thinking the same thing.

After they finished eating, April and Trevor ordered coffee and seemed to be content to linger. "I wish my dad had stayed in Saint Louis," April said, revealing what was uppermost on her mind.

"That's where you're from?" Nancy asked.

She nodded. "My father was on staff at one of the most respected medical school hospitals in the country. He was head of cardiology there until his heart condition prevented him from working." She smiled wistfully. "But he's a consultant to the state medical board of examiners, so I guess he's still a pretty important guy."

"Do you have any other family?" Ned asked.

"My mother died when I was little," she said. "I don't have any brothers or sisters."

"Neither do I," said Nancy. "And my father's a widower, too."

April asked about Nancy's father, and Nancy explained that he was a lawyer in River Heights.

"Does your father want you to become a lawyer, too?" April inquired.

"Oh, I don't know. I'm pretty happy with what I'm doing."

"What's that?"

"Didn't I tell you?" Trevor broke in. "Nancy's a detective. According to Ned, she's solved more cases than most detectives twice her age."

Nancy laughed. "Well, I wouldn't go that far."

"A detective?" April perked up. "That's great! Tell us about some of your cases."

Nancy entertained them with several of her more fascinating investigations, and as they listened, April and Trevor both seemed to forget their problems at the hospital. "And then there was the time that Ned got engaged to another girl just so he could find out what she was into," Nancy finished, giving Ned a friendly jab in the ribs. "And she ended up trying to push me out of the picture—permanently."

"What do you mean?"

"We went skydiving, and she sabotaged my parachute so it wouldn't open!"

April shivered. "Luckily, you survived!"

"Well, she actually saved me at the last minute. She was just trying to scare me."

"Detective work is so dangerous," said April. "You could get killed."

"Don't I know it," Ned said with feeling.

Then slowly Trevor's good mood evaporated as he became distracted and quiet, staring off into space.

As they drove back to the medical school, Nancy turned to Trevor. "Do you have to live at the school when you're in residency?" she asked.

"No, I have my own apartment. But sometimes it's easier just to stay in a dorm. I've had to work double shifts when we're understaffed."

"Double shifts. You mean sixteen hours? Don't you get tired?"

"You bet." As if to emphasize the point he stretched and yawned. "Last week was a real stress test. I'm exhausted."

"What happened in Room seven fifty-five tonight?" April asked Trevor quietly as Ned pulled up in front of her dorm.

Trevor stiffened. "What do you mean?"

"Why did Dr. Rayburn say there'd been a mistake?"

Nancy tried not to appear to be too interested, but she was curious. All evening she'd wanted to ask him about the patient who had nearly strangled to death.

Trevor took his time answering. "That patient was allergic to penicillin. There was red tape across the chart warning against prescribing it."

April looked puzzled. "So?"

"So apparently I prescribed penicillin anyway. The order was right on the patient's file in my handwriting! The patient was given the medicine orally. Her throat swelled up instantly. Her windpipe closed off. If I hadn't arrived when I did, she would have died. And it would have been *my fault!*"

Chapter

Three

"BUT HOW DID THAT HAPPEN?" April protested. "You must have seen the red tape!"

Trevor looked baffled and miserable. "I don't know how it happened. Mrs. Deverly, the patient, was admitted because of chest pains. She also had a slight infection, so an antibiotic was prescribed. I don't remember prescribing penicillin. But I know my own handwriting when I see it. And Dr. Rayburn saw it, too."

Nancy's mind was racing. She turned around to look at Trevor. "You were paged to Room seven fifty-five. By whom?"

"By one of the nurses." Trevor's eyes met

Nancy's. "I suppose Mrs. Deverly recognized her symptoms and called a nurse."

"Maybe the nurse or Mrs. Deverly can help explain the mix-up," Nancy suggested.

"And that's just what it is. A terrible mix-up," April declared. "No wonder you were upset."

Trevor shook his head soberly. "Mrs. Deverly was in shock and her heart stopped. Another couple of minutes and she could have died."

Nancy didn't blame Trevor for being shaken up. It was a serious mistake, and it appeared to have been Trevor's fault.

Ned dropped April and Trevor at the dorm. Both were quiet as they said good night to Nancy and Ned. April insisted that they all get together again while Ned was in town.

Afterward, while Ned was driving her home, Nancy was quiet and thoughtful. "What are you thinking?" he asked as they pulled into the Drews' driveway.

"That scene at the hospital was really scary tonight. Being a doctor sure means taking on a lot of responsibility."

Ned agreed. "What do you think about that prescription mix-up?"

"I think doctors can't afford to make that kind of mistake. It could be fatal."

"For what it's worth, Nancy, Trevor's not

irresponsible. I mean, I've known him a long time. All he's ever wanted is to be a good doctor. The best. He wouldn't prescribe the wrong medication. He would double-check."

Nancy nodded. Her impression of Trevor had been the same. He seemed conscientious, concerned, and caring. But there was always an element of human error in anything.

"Will I see you tomorrow?" Ned asked as he walked Nancy to the door.

Nancy laughed, gave him a quick kiss, and slipped inside the house. "How about noon at the hospital cafeteria? Maybe I'll treat you!" she threw over her shoulder.

"Some treat." Ned laughed, grimacing.

The sun was shining as Nancy drove up the winding road to Westmoor University Medical School. She pulled into the parking lot, searching for a spot near the main hospital entrance. The lot was nearly full, so she had to circle around toward the back entrance and squeeze into a narrow slot near the emergency room.

Once inside the hospital, Nancy found her way to the cafeteria with the help of red lines painted on the floor.

Nancy didn't see Ned, but she was hungry and decided to go ahead and order. "I'll take a

21

cheeseburger and fries," she told the girl behind the glass case.

Nancy was heading for a small table near a window when she saw April. She was standing and talking to a young man in a white lab coat. Nancy walked up behind the older girl.

"Hey, it's not my fault," the guy in the lab coat was saying. "Your old man got sick all on his own!"

Nancy had been about to speak, but the man's rudeness stopped her cold. She stared over April's shoulder at him.

"You had no business in CCU!" April replied in a shaky voice. "What were you trying to do?"

Nancy read the man's name tag: David Baines. He had no title so she assumed he was a volunteer or an orderly. He glared at Nancy through dark, angry eyes. "I was called in by the nurse, okay?" he snarled. "I was just doing my job."

"After that last incident, I told the nurse on duty to keep you away from my father. Don't you ever go near him again!"

"Fine, *Doctor* Shaw." He shouldered past April, knocking her into Nancy. Nancy scrambled to balance her tray, but some of her french fries tumbled to the floor anyway.

"Oh, Nancy," April said, flushing when she saw the damage. "I'm sorry. Let me help."

"No problem. I could do with a few less fries, anyway." She set the tray down on an unoccupied table, picked up the scattered fries, and disposed of them. Glancing at April, she asked, "Are you all right?"

April sighed and sank down into the seat opposite Nancy's. "You heard, huh?"

"Most of it."

"David Baines is a troublemaker," April declared angrily. "He's got a thing against doctors. You heard how he spoke to me! I don't know what his problem is, but I heard that he flunked out of med school and he resents anyone who's still in."

"I couldn't help overhearing you say something about 'that last incident,'" Nancy said, probing tentatively. "Do you mind my asking what happened?"

At that moment Ned called out, "There you are! Sorry I'm late." He appeared at their table, holding a tray piled with food. "My class ran over. Interesting stuff. I learned how each department in the hospital functions. It's amazing how many people work here. . . . Uh-oh, did I interrupt something?" he asked, apologizing.

"I just had an argument with one of the

hospital staff," April explained. She told Ned about David Baines, then added, "When my dad first came to visit, David must have seen us together. Apparently he knew my dad was a doctor. After my dad had his heart attack, David made a remark about how the 'eminent Dr. Gerard Shaw must be as mortal as the rest of us after all.' "

"How awful!" Nancy exclaimed.

"It really upset me," April admitted. "That's why I don't want him anywhere near my father."

"I don't blame you," said Ned. "What a jerk."

"Aren't you having lunch?" Nancy asked April.

"I'm not hungry. Too worried, I guess. You see, my father has a degenerative heart disease, and it's only a matter of time before he dies. There's nothing anyone can really do for him now. He was doing a little better for a while, but now . . ." She shrugged helplessly. "I just wish he could get better or that it would all go away! It's so hard watching him suffer."

They were all subdued during the rest of their meal. April's depression was catching, and after she left to return to her classes, Nancy and Ned were both quiet.

"I guess I should be getting back, too," Ned said. "We're getting a quick tour of the hospital pharmacy and medical labs this afternoon."

"Mmmm—"

"Nancy?"

"Hmmm?"

"What are you thinking about?"

"April. Trevor. David Baines. Medicine. Dinner tonight at my house. With you." She sent him an expectant look.

"I'll be there," he said, grinning. "As soon as classes are over."

Later that evening Nancy and Ned were settled down in front of the television set in the den. Nancy was nestled against Ned's chest, smiling to herself. It was good to have him around. "I'm so glad you're home for a while," she said, voicing her thoughts.

Ned gave her a squeeze. "Me, too. This seminar is really interesting, but I can't decide whether I want to specialize in hospital administration or not. It's fascinating. I mean, some of the jobs these people have. Can you imagine working in pathology?"

"Cutting up bodies? Yuck." Nancy grimaced.

"The medical school has a dissecting lab where they actually work on human bodies."

"Say no more," Nancy said. "I get the picture."

"And you wouldn't believe it. There are underground tunnels leading between all the buildings. They're kind of creepy and poorly lit, like something out of a horror movie."

"Don't tell Bess!" Nancy laughed.

"No way. She'd never set foot inside a hospital again!" Ned's grin slowly faded. "I saw Trevor today, but he was too busy to talk. He was discussing something with Dr. Rayburn and it looked serious."

The telephone rang before Nancy could ask Ned more about what he might have overheard. She answered it. "Hello?"

"Nancy? It's Trevor."

"Oh, hi, Trevor. Ned's right here, I—"

"No, wait, Nancy. I need to talk to you." His voice was low and shaky. "Can you come to the hospital?"

Nancy sat up straighter. "Sure. What's wrong?"

"Nancy, April's father, Dr. Gerard Shaw, died tonight," he said, his voice barely audible.

"Oh, no! How's April?"

"She's okay. At least she's putting up a good front. She'd been preparing herself for a long time." Trevor hesitated. "But, Nancy, it happened so unexpectedly. There's bound to be an investigation."

"Investigation? What are you talking about?"

"I was in the room just moments before Dr. Shaw died, and he was fine! But something must have gone wrong. Nancy, the hospital's blaming me for Dr. Shaw's death!"

Chapter

Four

"Hurry, Ned," Nancy called as she ran up the steps to the front entrance of the hospital.

"I'll be right there. Just let me lock the car!"

Nancy didn't wait. She yanked open the door, then stopped for a moment, looking around. The hospital lobby looked much the same as it had the evening before.

Trevor was seated in the lobby, and he looked really upset.

"Nancy!" he said, obviously relieved to see her. He jumped to his feet at the same moment Ned entered the building. "Ned. I'm so glad you're both here."

"Tell us what happened. From the beginning," Nancy said.

Trevor nodded. "Let's go to the doctors' lounge. It's more private."

He led them downstairs to a basement room that served as a lounge. They sat at a table, where Trevor collapsed in his chair. He ran his fingers through his hair in frustration. "Everything was normal. I just went in to check on Dr. Shaw. The cardiac nurse was there. April's father was doing fine."

"Where's April now?" Nancy asked worriedly.

"With Dr. Rayburn and the chief of staff and one of the other residents."

"Why are you being blamed?" asked Ned. "As I understand it, Dr. Shaw was really ill."

"He was. But Dr. Clemmons—he's the resident at the meeting—checked Dr. Shaw's chart, and he claims I ordered the wrong medicine for April's father. Dr. Rayburn checked it, too. And it's true!"

"You mean Dr. Shaw died from what you prescribed?" asked Nancy.

"No. The cardiac nurse knew her stuff. She knew the medicine prescribed was dangerous and took the chart to Dr. Clemmons. Clemmons was going to check on Dr. Shaw and then contact me. But April's father was dead by the time Clemmons and the nurse returned to the room. It all looks really suspicious because I was the last person to see Dr. Shaw alive except for the cardiac nurse."

Nancy was thinking out loud. "Maybe I'm missing something. Couldn't Dr. Shaw just have died from his heart condition?"

Trevor turned hollow eyes on Nancy. "I hope so. But we need an autopsy to prove it. Maybe I ordered something else wrong. That's what Dr. Rayburn, the chief of staff, and April are discussing." He drew a long breath. "This can't be easy on April. And I'm scared, too. What if the autopsy proves I did something wrong? How can I be making these mistakes?" He leaned his head against the back of the chair and stared up at the ceiling, answering his own question. "I'm *not* making these mistakes. It's impossible! I would at least remember making them if I had."

"Then what's going on?" Ned asked.

"I wish I knew." Trevor sighed. He turned to Nancy. "Any way you look at it, I'm in real trouble. My reputation as a doctor is at stake." He swallowed. "Clemmons brought the word 'malpractice' up a couple of times. If I get blamed, I might as well kiss my entire career good-bye."

"Oh, no. It can't be that bad." Nancy tried to make him feel better.

"Can't it?" Trevor rubbed his hand over his face. Then he looked at Nancy, his expression brightening a little. "I asked you to come because you're a detective, Nancy. Do you think you could help clear my name?"

Nancy glanced at Ned, then back at Trevor. "I can try to find out how those prescription mix-ups happened."

"I'll need all the help I can get." Trevor smiled wearily. "Oh, by the way, I talked to Mrs. Deverly's nurse. Mrs. Deverly recognized her symptoms and realized that she'd been given penicillin; she'd been through it once before. She called the nurse, and the nurse in turn called me. Nothing more suspicious than that."

The door to the doctors' lounge opened, and April walked in. Her face was pale and drawn, her lips bloodless. Trevor stood up and tentatively took her arm. Nancy could tell he wasn't certain of his reception. After all, he'd practically been accused of causing her father's death!

April managed to pull herself together, forcing a weak smile for Nancy and Ned. "I don't want you to think I blame you," she said to Trevor. "I know it's not your fault."

Trevor gave her a big hug of relief. "Thanks" was all he said.

Ned cleared his throat as April and Trevor sat

down. "Trevor's asked Nancy to get to the bottom of this prescription mix-up," he informed April. "If anyone can do it, she can."

"Good," April said, distracted. "That's the important thing now."

The color was coming back to April's face, and Nancy could tell she was getting over the worst of her shock. Pretty fast, too, Nancy thought.

"I'm almost relieved it's over," April said as if reading Nancy's mind. "My dad suffered far too long. Now we can all get on with our lives. That's what he would have wanted."

"When's the autopsy to be done?" Trevor asked.

April's pretty face clouded. "I wouldn't grant permission for it. I know it's unprofessional of me, but I can't help it. We're talking about my own father's body."

Trevor stared at her in surprise. Nancy could almost guess what was going through his mind. If April didn't consent to the autopsy, Trevor's name would never be completely cleared!

"I think it's time to call it a night," Nancy said. "I'll start work on this first thing in the morning." She turned to Trevor. "How about if I meet you in the lobby around nine tomorrow?"

"Fine," Trevor murmured, but his gaze never left April's face.

* * *

The next morning Nancy arrived at the hospital promptly at nine. She wasn't certain what she could do to help, but she planned to ask Trevor's colleagues a few questions.

Trevor was waiting in the lobby, dressed in street clothes.

Nancy smiled. "I forgot you're not on duty at this hour. Sorry. We could have made it later."

"Forget it. I'm so anxious to clear my name, I'd work around the clock if necessary." He grimaced. "I ran into Dr. Rayburn this morning and he was pretty upset. I've made two critical mistakes in two days. I feel as if I'm walking on eggshells."

"Can you give me an hour-by-hour replay of your last few days? Since the day before Mrs. Deverly was given the wrong medication?"

"I'll try," he said.

They walked outside, taking a path through the park that separated the hospital from the cliff high above the river. Trevor was quite open and so detailed that by the end of a few hours Nancy was convinced that he'd accounted for every minute.

"Whew!" she said at last. "Most people wouldn't be able to account for their actions in such detail." Nancy realized that Trevor had an uncommonly good memory. How could someone like that make the kind of errors he'd been accused of? It didn't seem possible.

Back at the hospital Trevor went to the cafeteria in search of April. Though it was lunchtime, Nancy headed straight to the cardiology floor. She wanted to ask some questions about Trevor. Nancy stopped a young nurse on the seventh floor and engaged her in conversation.

"Oh, you want to know about Trevor." The nurse smiled knowingly. "Sorry, he's taken already. He's engaged to one of the medical students. I think her name's April."

"I've met April," Nancy said, hiding a smile. "I just wanted to know what Trevor's like to work with."

"The best. He's fun, and he works hard. And he doesn't order the nurses and staff around. He's really great." She looked a little wistful.

Nancy smiled to herself as she headed for the elevators. Well, Trevor had at least one loyal fan!

She took the elevator downstairs, and when the doors opened on the first floor, Nancy nearly stepped right into April and Trevor.

"There you are!" Trevor said, clearly pleased to see Nancy. "April's got only a few minutes before she has to be in class, but she wanted to tell you something."

"What?"

April looked down at her hands. "I thought

you should know that I've agreed to the autopsy after all. Not that I think there's any reason for it," she said quickly. "I'm sure my father died of natural causes. But if it'll help prove no one was at fault, then I guess it's necessary." She turned her gaze on her fiancé. "But I do hate the idea."

Trevor nodded understandingly. He looked at Nancy. "They're taking April's father's body from the morgue to the pathology lab. I think I'll check to make sure things go smoothly."

Nancy realized Trevor was trying to make April feel better. "May I come with you? I haven't seen the pathology department."

"Are you sure you're up to it?" Trevor asked.

"Lead on, Doctor." Nancy smiled.

Nancy and Trevor took the elevator down to the basement. The elevator doors clanged open, revealing a narrow cinder-block hallway painted off-white.

Trevor walked briskly, apparently as anxious as Nancy to get this over with. The words "Hospital Morgue" loomed ahead, painted in black letters on a door at the end of the hall. Trevor pushed against the door. Nervously, Nancy followed. Against one wall was a row of built-in steel cabinets. The morgue itself was neat, tidy, and cold. Only the stinging scent of formaldehyde and the low temperature reminded Nancy of where they were.

"Hi, Glen," Trevor said to the man seated at a desk in the corner. "This is Nancy Drew. Nancy, meet Glen Waters. Glen's in charge down here."

"Hi. What can I do you for?" Glen grinned widely.

"It's kind of delicate," Trevor admitted. "Dr. Gerard Shaw's body was brought down yesterday. He's my fiancée's father, and I promised I'd just check to make sure everything's okay."

"Yeah. That one's scheduled for a postmortem," Glen remarked. "I'm sending it over today."

He walked over to the row of steel cabinets. Nancy knew the cabinets held bodies. She drew in a breath as Glen grabbed the handle of a drawer marked "Gerard Shaw."

The drawer slid open. The cabinet was empty!

Chapter

Five

Glen stared in amazement. "But that's impossible!" he sputtered. "I put the body in here myself. Someone's taken it!"

"What?" Trevor demanded.

"I tell you, I put the body in this drawer last night!" Glen insisted.

"Well, then, where is it?"

"I don't know!"

"Who else works here?" asked Nancy, trying to calm them both.

Glen blinked several times. "Well, Sam Hughes works the night shift now. I just switched

today to days, so I relieved him this morning.
There's another guy on the afternoon shift. But
he hasn't worked since Dr. Shaw's body was
brought down. Sam's the only other person who
could have moved it."

Glen reached for his desk phone and called
Sam at home. It was clear from Glen's side of the
conversation that Sam didn't know what Glen
was talking about.

Replacing the receiver, Glen frowned. "Sam
says nobody touched that drawer while he was
working. And he only left the morgue once, to get
a sandwich from the vending machine. He always
does that. He locked the door when he left, as he
always does."

Nancy shared a look with Trevor. "Could the
body just be misplaced?" she asked Glen.

"No way. But if it'll make you feel better, I'll
look in every drawer to make sure. Shaw's body
has to be somewhere!"

"What will I tell April?" Trevor murmured as
they headed back upstairs. "If Glen doesn't find
Dr. Shaw's body, I'll have to inform the chief of
staff."

Trevor left Nancy, intending to track April
down in class and tell her the upsetting news.
Nancy grabbed a sandwich from a vending machine, then rode the elevator to the seventh floor.
She hoped to catch Dr. Rayburn. He might be

able to explain more about what had happened to Dr. Shaw's body.

Nancy recognized Dr. Rayburn standing outside one of the patients' rooms, his nose buried in a chart. "Dr. Rayburn?" she asked.

He lifted his brows inquiringly.

Nancy introduced herself, adding, "Trevor has asked me to help clear his name. He's afraid a malpractice suit could ruin his career."

"Trevor's right," Dr. Rayburn said regretfully. "But I don't see how you can help, Ms. Drew. The medical board of examiners looks into these things. The decision about Trevor's future as a doctor is in their hands. After the autopsy's performed, I'm sure his name will be cleared."

Nancy had just about concluded her interview when a man in a guard's uniform approached her. "Are you Ms. Drew?" he asked.

"Yes."

"The chief of staff would like to see you in the conference room. I'll take you there now, if it's all right."

"Thank you."

Dr. Wicks, the chief of staff, was a white-haired gentleman with a deeply furrowed brow. Trevor was with him in the spacious oblong room when Nancy arrived. He shot her a nervous glance.

"Ms. Drew," Dr. Wicks began without preamble, "I understand you were with Dr. Callahan when he discovered that Dr. Shaw's body was missing."

"That's correct."

"I don't mean to be abrupt, but this is a confidential hospital matter. I'd like to keep it as such."

"I have no intention of talking to the press," Nancy assured him. "I just would like to help April and Trevor."

Dr. Wicks's attitude warmed somewhat. "I'm certain the problem will be resolved shortly. Please, sit down." He gestured toward the chairs tucked snugly beneath the polished table. "I've been informed you've been asking questions about Dr. Callahan, Ms. Drew, and that you've been working in an unofficial capacity to help him avoid a malpractice suit. You're not a member of the hospital staff, and it's highly irregular to have you asking questions at all."

Nancy opened her mouth to defend herself, but she had no time to follow through. Dr. Wicks leaned across the table and said, "I, for one, would be interested to hear what you've learned. Why don't you start from the beginning and tell me what's been going on?"

Two hours later Nancy and Trevor left the conference room. Trevor seemed dazed. "Well, he didn't say you couldn't help me," he said. "That's something."

"Yeah, but I've got to find a way to be less conspicuous," Nancy reminded him. "What do you think I should do?"

It was nearly time to meet April and Ned, so they headed directly to the cafeteria, where they'd agreed to rendezvous.

"How about becoming a candy striper?" Trevor suggested as they pushed through the door.

"A candy striper!" Nancy repeated and laughed.

"There you are," April called out, obviously relieved. White-faced, she hurried toward them, Ned in tow. "How could my father's body be missing?" she asked in a quavering voice. "What's happening at this hospital?"

Trevor put his arm around her shoulders. "I don't know. But it's clear to me that someone's out to get me."

Nancy didn't comment. She wasn't as convinced as Trevor seemed to be that he was the prime target. Whoever had moved Dr. Shaw's body was taking an enormous risk. If someone was trying to destroy Trevor's career, there were easier ways. "How do I become a candy striper for a few days?" she asked.

Ned cocked an eyebrow at her. "A candy striper? Oh, Nancy, I can hardly wait."

Nancy smiled, glad to have lightened the mood.

"I can tell the supervisor in charge and she'll sign you on," said Trevor. "We always need volunteers. Just go to Madeleine Creyton's office tomorrow morning."

"Where's that?"

"It's in the administration building," Ned explained. "The small building next to this one."

"You're sure learning the geography," Nancy teased, linking arms with him.

"Hey." He humbly lifted his palms. "Can I help it if I'm an A student? Go ahead, ask me anything."

"Where's the school's anatomy lab?" April asked, relaxing a bit.

"Ummm." Ned squeezed his eyes shut in concentration. "The medical school classroom building. The older ivy-covered building right above the river. It used to be the hospital before this structure was built."

"Pretty good. Which floor?"

"Fifth?"

April smiled. "The medical school is only three stories high."

"Oh."

Nancy laughed. "Two out of three's not bad. Come on, take me home and feed me or lose me forever."

"Are you sure there're only three floors?" Ned grumbled as Nancy tugged him toward the door.

"Positive," April called after him.

Nancy gave Ned a quick peck on the cheek as soon as they were outside.

"And what was that for?" he asked, drawing Nancy into his arms.

"For shaking off some of April's depression. And—because I like you."

"That's it? You just *like* me?"

Nancy laughed and pulled him toward her car. "What do you think?"

Wednesday morning Nancy was at the hospital promptly at seven, in time to work the first shift of the day. At Trevor's suggestion, she'd worn a pair of white tennis shoes. She'd also done her hair in a French braid.

She found Madeleine Creyton's office and was given a pile of forms to fill out as well as a candy striper uniform. "Dr. Callahan told us to expect you," the supervisor said with a friendly smile.

"Thanks."

"Report to the emergency room. Normally, we don't have candy stripers working there, but we're really shortstaffed this week. Dr. Callahan assured me you could handle it."

Nancy wasn't so sure. Emergency? She had visions of people coming in covered with blood. Sighing, she headed back to the hospital. She wasn't sure she wanted to be a candy striper. When would she find the time for detecting?

The emergency room was quiet when Nancy walked in. She introduced herself and was handed a clipboard and a stack of forms. "We need you to take down information as patients come in," the head nurse told her. "Don't worry. Most of the day cases are pretty minor. The late-night accidents are the worst."

There was no time during her break to do any investigating, but at lunchtime Nancy made a dash through the cafeteria, grabbed a sandwich, then headed for the double doors.

"Whoa!" Ned exclaimed when she barreled into him. "Where are you going? Aren't we eating together?"

"Sorry. I've got to use every spare minute to learn who's out to ruin Trevor's reputation."

"Well, where are you going?" His gaze swept over her. "You know, you look kind of cute."

"Thanks a lot." Nancy grinned. "Actually, I'd like to take a look at those patients' charts on which Trevor supposedly prescribed the wrong medicines. Do you know where Dr. Shaw's chart would be now?"

"Uh, no. Ask the ward clerk at the seventh-floor nurses' station. She ought to know."

"Okay." A teasing light sparkled in her eyes. "You know, for someone who thinks hospital food isn't fit for consumption, I notice you're here in the cafeteria a lot."

"Hey, bad food is better than no food."

Laughing, Nancy headed for the elevators. The seventh-floor ward clerk wasn't sure where Dr. Shaw's file was. "I doubt it's down in medical records yet. Check with Dr. Rayburn. His office is down the hall and around the corner. He and Dr. Callahan and Dr. Clemmons were discussing the case."

Nancy headed in the direction the ward clerk had pointed; Rayburn's office was easy to find. Nancy rapped on the gray door, but there was no answer. Twisting the handle, she found it unlocked.

A woman was just rising from a desk, straightening papers. "Sorry," she said. "I was just finishing some work before lunch, and I didn't answer the door right away. Did you want to see Dr. Rayburn? He's not in, but you can leave him a message. I'm his secretary."

Nancy was in the anteroom of a two-room office. Plush pearl gray carpeting swept across the floor and into the adjacent room, Dr. Rayburn's office. Nancy glanced toward his open office door. "Will he be long?" she asked.

"I'm not certain."

"May I wait a few minutes? I'm on my lunch break, too. I'd really like to see him."

Hesitating, Rayburn's secretary finally shrugged her shoulders. "Okay. I won't be long." She discreetly closed Rayburn's office door before she went to lunch.

Nancy waited a few minutes, then grew anxious about all the time she was wasting. All she really wanted to know was if Dr. Rayburn had Dr. Shaw's or Mrs. Deverly's file.

She tried the door to his office. Locked. Seeing the keyhole in the knob, Nancy knew it would be an easy lock to pick. She pulled a hairpin from her braid and stuck it into the keyhole. The lock button popped open. Nancy noiselessly pushed open the door and slipped inside.

Rayburn's desk stood in the center of the spacious room. A brass coatrack occupied one corner, and one paneled wall was covered with an impressive display of medical diplomas and awards. Nancy's gaze zeroed in on a short stack of narrow three-ring binders—the kind used for patients' charts—sitting on a counter beneath the window.

Nancy quickly searched through the binders. Mrs. Deverly's was on the bottom. Aha! she thought excitedly, pulling it out.

Across the front of the binder was a piece of red tape with Allergic printed in white letters over and over again across its face. It was impossible to miss!

Quickly Nancy leafed through the papers clipped to the top of the binder. A shuffling noise startled her and she glanced over her shoulder. No one there.

Nerves, she thought, hurriedly scanning the pages. A smaller white page labeled Standard Orders was on top. "Penicillin" was handwritten on the sheet, plain as day, followed by the initials *TC.*

"There it is as big as life," Nancy murmured unhappily. She stared at the chart, wishing she knew enough about medicine to understand all the codes on the page. Trevor's initials appeared several more times.

Another creaking sound sent a shiver of alarm up Nancy's spine. She whirled around. Her eyes widened. Someone dressed completely in green surgical garb was charging straight at her!

"Hey!" Nancy screamed. Hands encased in plastic surgical gloves covered her mouth. Nancy tried to scream again.

To her horror she felt something jab into her upper arm. A hypodermic needle!

"Help me!" she yelled against the smothering fingers, but it was too late. Blackness descended over her. She slipped limply into unconsciousness, the binder dropping from her fingers.

Chapter

Six

NANCY! NANCY! Please, wake up! *Nancy!*"
Nancy heard her name being called far in the
distance. Her ears buzzed and her tongue felt too
big for her mouth. She swallowed, then tried to
form words.

"Nancy? Look, she's coming around!" the
same voice cried in relief.

It was Ned's voice, Nancy realized. She
couldn't open her eyes. Her eyelids felt weighted
down.

"Give her this." Nancy heard Trevor's voice.

She was lifted into a sitting position, a paper
cup placed against her mouth. Some liquid

slipped between her lips, and she swallowed automatically. It was water. Slowly, she opened her eyes.

"Where am I?" she asked, confused, not recognizing her surroundings.

"You're in one of the patients' rooms," Trevor said. "A nurse found you in the stairwell. We were taking you to the E.R. when you started to stir, so we brought you here instead. What happened? Did you fall?"

Slowly Nancy focused on Trevor. He was standing at the foot of the hospital bed. Ned was holding her shoulders, his dark eyes worriedly searching her face.

"Fall?" Nancy repeated on a short laugh. "No, I didn't fall. I was attacked!" She turned her arm so the small red mark was visible where the hypodermic needle had pricked her skin. "I think I'm lucky to be alive," she added soberly.

"*What?*" Trevor grabbed hold of her arm, staring in disbelief at the small puncture wound. The color drained from his face. "Someone did this to you on purpose?"

"I was in Dr. Rayburn's office, looking at the Deverly file. Someone ran in dressed in surgical greens and mask. I've got to get that file!" Nancy struggled to her feet, remembering.

"Slow down!" Ned warned, gently pushing her

down onto the bed. "Someone just shot you with a hypodermic. You need to be checked out!"

"I know, but I need that file. I'm sure that's why I was attacked."

"I'll go back to Rayburn's office and get the file," Trevor said. "Ned, take Nancy down to the lab. I'll call and order some blood tests."

An hour later Nancy was pronounced fit to leave. She'd been injected with a common sedative, which had no serious side effects.

"I still think you should go home," Ned said worriedly.

"Trust me. I'm fine. Besides, you're the one who has to explain why you missed your class."

"Are you Nancy Drew?" one of the lab nurses asked as they were about to leave.

"Yes."

"Dr. Callahan just called. He asked you to meet him in the doctors' lounge in the basement if you feel up to it."

"Thanks."

"I'm coming with you," Ned insisted.

"No, Ned. You go back to your class. I'll talk to Trevor. I'm fine. Really." She squeezed his arm, heading for the door.

Grumbling under his breath, he muttered to the room at large, "There's no talking to her."

Trevor was seated at one of the tables, and April was with him. "I begged off my classes this afternoon," April admitted. "I can't concentrate right now."

Nancy smiled sympathetically. "What about—" she began, but stopped in midsentence when Trevor shook his head.

"The Deverly file wasn't in Dr. Rayburn's office. In fact, it seems to be missing entirely. Dr. Rayburn is really upset about everything. He's furious that you were in his office and that someone purposely sedated you. And he's fit to be tied about the missing file." Trevor grimaced. "The chief of staff's in a real state, too. We had to order a new file made up."

Nancy hoped Dr. Wicks wouldn't pull her off the case. It was certainly within his power. "Whoever attacked me didn't want me to see that file."

"Then it won't surprise you that Dr. Shaw's file is missing, too," Trevor added. "I told you, Nancy—it's a plot. Someone's trying to ruin my career!"

This time Nancy didn't argue. Someone *had* attacked her. And that meant someone thought she was a threat. "Who would want to ruin your career?" Nancy asked. "Have you got any enemies?"

April and Trevor quickly exchanged looks, but

neither responded right away. "Well, maybe," he said finally.

"Who?"

"Suzanne Welles," April answered for him. "She's an administrator here at the hospital, and she—uh—doesn't really like Trevor—or me."

Nancy asked, "Why?"

"Suzanne and I were dating," Trevor explained. "We were pretty serious for a while. Then she talked about getting married, but I didn't think I was ready. We broke up, and then right after that, I met April." He shot his fiancée a quick, affectionate glance. "The rest is history," he added softly.

"Do you think she would carry a grudge this far?" Nancy asked skeptically. "I mean, not only is Trevor's reputation suffering, but whoever's changing the patients' charts is also endangering their lives. That's criminal."

Trevor seemed to consider. "No, I don't think so," he answered. "Suzanne's angry, but she's not vindictive. She wouldn't risk patients' lives or her career."

April opened her mouth, then clamped it shut again; clearly she had wanted to disagree with Trevor. Nancy sensed the hostility April felt for Suzanne. She wasn't sure what to believe, but she made a mental note to find Suzanne Welles as soon as possible.

Nancy left a few minutes later to check at the administration building to find out where Suzanne worked. She learned Suzanne had her own office on the fourth floor.

Nancy took the elevator and stepped out into a hallway. A dark gray carpet deadened the sound of her steps. The lighting was indirect and tasteful. Unlike the hospital, which was designed for efficiency, the administration building—at least this floor—was decorated for comfort.

Suzanne's name was embossed on a bronze nameplate recessed in the oak door. Nancy knocked softly, and a young woman let her in.

"Yes?" she inquired politely, taking in Nancy's candy striper uniform.

"I'm looking for Suzanne Welles," Nancy explained. "My name is Nancy Drew. Are you Suzanne?"

"I'm Suzanne's secretary," the young woman explained. "Do you have an appointment?"

Nancy hadn't understood the importance of Suzanne's position. It was clear Suzanne was high up to be awarded such a luxurious office and her own secretary. "No. I'm a friend of Dr. Trevor Callahan's."

The young woman hesitated, then shrugged and lifted the receiver on her phone. She explained who Nancy was to the person on the other end.

"Go right in," the secretary said, her voice tinged with surprise.

"Thank you." Nancy opened the door to Suzanne Welles's office.

A woman in her twenties sat in a leather chair behind a massive oak desk. Her dark hair was swept up, and the suit she wore was simple and expensive.

"All right, Nancy Drew," she said. "What's your angle?"

Her directness surprised Nancy. "Angle?"

"I have a budget meeting in fifteen minutes with the administrative director. I don't have time to waste. What have you got to do with Trevor Callahan?"

"Maybe I should come back another time," Nancy murmured.

"Did Trevor send you?"

"No, I—" Nancy stopped to collect herself. Suzanne Welles certainly had a way of making her feel ill at ease! "Trevor said you're a friend of his," Nancy spoke up, deciding to fight fire with fire. She could be as direct and bold as Suzanne. "He's in trouble now, and I thought you could help."

"What kind of trouble? And how are you involved?" Suzanne drew her brows together.

Nancy quickly explained everything. Suzanne visibly softened.

"But Trevor didn't actually ask for my help, did he?" she guessed. Sighing, she said, "Okay, let me be honest. I thought I was in love with Trevor once, but I wasn't. That's over."

"You don't know anyone who might want to hurt him?"

Suzanne's face flushed. "Is that why you're here? Because you think I want revenge?" She rose, crossed the room, and opened the door. It was a clear invitation to leave, and Nancy reluctantly turned toward the outer office.

"If someone's making mistakes, it might be Trevor himself, you know," Suzanne said. "He's the most logical choice, isn't he?"

She closed the door behind Nancy with more force than was necessary.

It was late afternoon by the time Nancy returned to her post in the emergency room. Her head was swimming with thoughts of Suzanne Welles. She was certain Suzanne still had feelings for Trevor, no matter what she said. Why else would Suzanne have agreed to see her unless she hoped Trevor had sent Nancy as a way of breaking the ice between them again? When Suzanne had seen that Nancy was merely trying to help Trevor, her hopes had obviously been dashed, although she'd tried to deny her feelings.

She must still love Trevor. But how could she be involved in ruining his reputation? She had seemed genuinely concerned for Trevor until she found out why Nancy was there.

In the emergency room, a young girl in a softball uniform was slumped in a chair beside her mother. The sticker on her T-shirt said her name was Carla. Nancy smiled at her and asked, "Can you fill this form out?"

Carla lifted her left hand, pointing to her right one. "I can't," she said, heaving a huge sigh. Her right hand was wrapped in a white terry-cloth towel.

"We think Carla's finger is broken," the woman beside her said, taking the clipboard from Nancy.

"I might be out for the season!" Carla wailed.

"Maybe it's not that bad," Nancy said consolingly. She stared at the sticker on the girl's T-shirt, and something clicked inside her head. White sticker. Penicillin. "Excuse me," she said, striding toward the emergency room desk. On top of the counter were several patients' binders. Nancy opened one. A chart had just been started. A white paper marked Standard Orders lay on top, the patient's name typed across the page.

"Hey, Nancy! I thought your shift ended at three."

"Ned!" she cried excitedly, grabbing his arm, and dragging him toward an empty corner of the emergency room.

"Well, if I'd known I was going to get this warm a reception, I would have been here sooner," he teased.

"It gets better." Nancy's eyes sparkled. "I just figured out how someone tampered with Trevor's patients' files!"

Chapter

Seven

N ED STARED AT HER in amazement. "You did? How?"

"I got a quick look at Mrs. Deverly's file this morning before I was attacked. On the doctor's Standard Orders page Mrs. Deverly's name was on one of those white labels stuck on the chart. Normally the patient's name is typed on. Don't you see? Someone *covered up* the real name. Trevor's orders weren't for Mrs. Deverly at all!"

Ned whistled.

"Those orders were for some other patient," Nancy went on. "That's why Trevor's handwriting was on it! Someone substituted those orders into Mrs. Deverly's file. Trevor had really ordered penicillin for another patient!"

"Wow." Ned shook his head. "But what about the red tape warning against an allergic reaction?"

"It had to have been ripped from the file and later replaced."

"But weren't Trevor's orders dated?" Ned asked, thinking fast. "They date everything around here."

"I bet the dates were altered, too. Those orders could have been for any patient since Trevor's been a resident. No one really looked at the dates. It was Trevor's handwriting on the file *ordering* the penicillin that put everything in an uproar."

"Nancy"—Ned gripped her arm—"if what you're saying is true, then some maniac is running around the hospital switching files!"

"Switching *Trevor's* files, and putting patients' lives in danger! He or she is after Trevor."

Ned nodded, his handsome face grave. "Why would anyone be out to get Trevor?"

Nancy thought of Suzanne. "I don't know," she said quietly. "And what about Dr. Shaw's body? Whoever took it must have had a powerful motive. I can't believe it hasn't turned up by now."

They headed for the seventh floor to look for Trevor in cardiology. As they rounded a corner, Nancy nearly ran into David Baines. The surly orderly was trying to follow Dr. Rayburn into his office.

"Excuse me, Mr. Baines," Rayburn said patiently but firmly. "I have work to do."

"Work to do. Right. Like in Saint Louis?" David asked, his tone nasty. He anxiously twirled a set of keys around one finger.

Rayburn just shook his head and strode into his office. David, noticing Nancy and Ned for the first time, said with a short laugh, "Well, if it isn't the girl detective and her flunky."

Ned bristled, but Nancy put a hand on his arm. "Who told you I was a detective?" she asked David.

"No one had to tell me. You're asking all kinds of questions about Trevor Callahan." He twirled the keys again before he walked past them.

"Did you see those keys?" Ned demanded. "Those were Porsche keys. I recognized them."

"Porsche keys," Nancy repeated, staring down the empty hallway where David had disappeared. "Tell me, how can an orderly afford a Porsche?"

"I don't know," Ned replied thoughtfully.

Ten minutes later they found Trevor in Room 721, speaking with a young boy whose chest was bandaged. Trevor was holding a soccer ball and smiling at his patient. "So, you're a soccer player," he was saying. "How long have you been playing?"

"A few years." The boy plucked at his sheets. "I won't play this year."

"Oh, you never know. You've got six months until fall season. You'll be as good as new by then." He glanced over his shoulder, spying Nancy and Ned in the doorway. "Be back later," he told the boy with a wink.

"What's up?" he asked, joining them in the corridor.

Trevor listened attentively while Nancy told him about her theory regarding the altered charts. "Nancy, you're fantastic! So *that's* how it was done!"

"We don't know for certain," Nancy reminded him. "It's just a theory."

"I'm going straight to the chief of staff to straighten this out," Trevor said, already in motion.

"Trevor, I—"

"Catch you later," he yelled, running through the closing doors of the elevator.

"Now what?" Ned asked.

Nancy pushed back a strand of hair from her face. The way Trevor jumped to conclusions made her uneasy. "How about food?" she suggested.

"You read my mind. But let's get out of this place, okay?"

"Okay."

They rode the elevator down to the first floor and headed for the exit. Ned held the door, and the cool evening air stirred Nancy's hair.

"You know, I should talk to April before we leave," Nancy said. "I want to know more about David Baines."

Ned clutched his stomach as if he might die of starvation.

Nancy laughed. "Bring the car around to the front of the hospital. I'll be right back. I promise."

"Okay."

Nancy walked quickly down the corridor toward the front desk. It was quite possible April had already left for the day, and if so, Nancy was going to have to call her dorm room.

"Could you page Dr. April Shaw?" she asked the woman wearing the headset.

Recognizing Nancy, the woman smiled and complied. Within moments a call came back through. "Dr. Shaw's in the cafeteria, Ms. Drew. She asked you to join her."

When Nancy entered the cafeteria, she found April seated in the corner, an untouched plate of food pushed aside. She was holding a photograph in her hands as Nancy sat down beside her.

"Hi," Nancy said, looking at the photograph. "How're you doing?"

"This is a picture of my dad." She handed it to Nancy. Tears suddenly filled her blue eyes. "It's all so terrible," she said, her voice cracking. Suddenly she covered her face with both hands and sobbed. All the emotion she'd been bottling up came pouring out. "I feel so guilty!"

"April, I'm really sorry about your father," Nancy murmured softly.

"No. No." She shook her head, sniffing. "I miss him, but his death was a blessing. Now it's Trevor I'm worried about."

"Listen, don't worry about Trevor. Everything will be fine as soon as I—"

"You don't understand." April dropped her hands, staring at Nancy through scared, tear-drenched eyes. "I think—I think . . ." She stopped, as if she couldn't go on.

"You think what?" Nancy probed gently.

"Nancy, I think Trevor's got serious problems. It *is* his fault that my father's body is missing! He's the one making the mistakes!"

Nancy stared at April in disbelief. "What do you mean?"

"These things that have happened—they're not coincidences. There's only one explanation that makes sense: Trevor arranged everything!

We only have his word that he didn't." April's eyes swam with fresh tears.

She's really distressed and not thinking clearly, Nancy thought. "April, listen to me. I think I know how Trevor's patients' charts were tampered with." Quietly and calmly she explained her theory.

But April shook her head. "Nancy, there's more." With a supreme effort, April collected herself. People at other tables were starting to stare, and she pulled a tissue from her pocket and dabbed at her eyes. "Nancy, the CCU nurse reported a conversation she overheard between Trevor and my father. My father was depressed, and he told Trevor it would be better if he just died. Nancy, he even suggested *ways* Trevor could arrange it."

"The CCU nurse told you this?" Nancy asked quickly.

April nodded. "Uh-huh. She reported it to Dr. Rayburn, too. What if Trevor did kill my father?" she asked in a low, shaky voice. "Oh, Nancy, what if Trevor thought he was doing me and my dad a favor?"

Chapter

Eight

Nancy wanted to cover her ears. She'd just seen what a wonderful doctor Trevor was. Could what April was suggesting be true?

"Maybe that's why he's hidden the body," April said, clapping her hand over her mouth in distress. "He's afraid an autopsy will reveal the truth!"

"You're talking murder, April," Nancy warned quietly. "A mercy killing is still murder."

"I know," she murmured miserably. "Why do you think I'm scared to death?"

Ten minutes later Nancy walked April through the cool spring evening to her dorm. She signaled to Ned, indicating through hand motions where she was headed. Ned turned on his lights and drove ahead of them toward the dorm.

April was like a zombie. "You don't have to baby-sit with me, Nancy."

"You're in no condition to be alone tonight. Are you sure you don't want me to stay?"

"No, there're a lot of people in the dorm. And Trevor will stop by later." She sighed heavily. "I don't know what I'm going to say to him."

Realizing April had half convinced herself of Trevor's guilt, Nancy saw it was becoming even more important to find out who had tampered with the files. I've just got to find them, figure out who did it, and *why,* she thought. Then Nancy remembered something she had wanted to ask April. "I ran into David Baines today," she said. "Does he drive a Porsche?"

"Umm. I don't know. No, wait a minute. Somebody said something about a red sports car. I think he does drive a Porsche." She stared blankly at Nancy. "Why?"

"Well, how can he afford one on an orderly's salary? Does he have another job?"

"I don't know."

Nancy tried another tack. "I overheard him say something about Saint Louis to Dr. Rayburn this afternoon. Didn't you say your father was from Saint Louis?"

"Oh, I know what that's about," April answered. "Saint Louis is where David flunked out of med school. He told one of the staff he got thrown out by mistake, but knowing David, I doubt it."

"Is that how he knew your father was a doctor?" Nancy was fishing, but she thought there might be some connection. "Could that be why David was so bitter toward him? Because your father taught at the med school that tossed him out?"

"Maybe."

They stopped in front of the door to the dorm. "Thanks, Nancy," April said with a small smile. "See you tomorrow."

On Thursday morning Nancy smiled as she parked her car near the emergency room entrance. The now familiar buildings of Westmoor University Medical School looked solid and secure, not like the home of the mad killers who had filled Nancy's dreams.

Spotting the reflection of her pink and white uniform in the hospital's glass door, Nancy made a face. She had to find time away from her candy striper duties to do some investigating.

She'd barely begun recording new patient information when Trevor appeared. He was in jeans and an open-collared shirt. "Nancy," he said. "Could I talk to you?"

"Sure." She gave him a quick look. His voice was strained, and he looked as though he hadn't shaved that morning. "You're here awfully early."

"I didn't sleep at all last night. What's wrong with April? She would hardly talk to me."

Nancy sighed. "Trevor, I need to ask you some questions," she said delicately, realizing he could easily take what she was about to say the wrong way.

"Ask away."

"Well, I was talking to April, and apparently one of the CCU nurses overheard a conversation between you and April's father."

"What kind of conversation?"

Nancy explained to Trevor what April had told her, finishing with "The nurse apparently reported the conversation to Dr. Rayburn."

At Nancy's abrupt silence, Trevor glanced away. "I remember. Lots of patients talk like that, Nancy. They get depressed. You have to encourage them, and as they get better, they get over their depression."

"But, Trevor, we're talking about a patient who suggested a mercy killing!"

A dark flush moved up Trevor's neck. "It

wasn't like that." His gray eyes fixed on Nancy's for the first time since she had made her suggestion. "You don't seriously believe I would perform a mercy killing, do you?"

"No. I don't."

"But someone else does, right? Who?" Trevor demanded, growing angry. "Who said that? Dr. Rayburn? He knows I'd never do anything like that!"

Nancy hardly knew what to say.

"No, wait. I get it. You talked to Suzanne yesterday, didn't you? She somehow found out about that conversation. She won't leave me alone."

"It wasn't Suzanne," Nancy admitted reluctantly, "although I do need to talk to you about her."

"Then who was it?" Trevor demanded, ignoring Nancy's attempts to divert the conversation. At Nancy's continued silence his face slowly changed. "Oh, no. Not April." He looked shocked.

"April's upset about her father," Nancy said hurriedly. "I think she's been hiding her feelings, trying to bury them. It didn't work and now she's a wreck. She said she even feels guilty."

"Nancy." Trevor's eyes were full of pain and disbelief. "Does April believe I killed her father? Is that why she was so distant last night?"

How do I get myself into these things? Nancy wondered unhappily. "She knows you love her, and she thought maybe, because you knew how much it hurt her to see her father suffer . . ." She trailed off, not wanting to hurt Trevor further.

Trevor stared at Nancy for several moments, then slowly climbed to his feet. He left without saying goodbye. Nancy felt terrible. She went back to work, but could hardly concentrate. When Glen Waters called from the morgue, she listened only halfheartedly.

"Hey, look, security really tore this place apart from top to bottom. Dr. Shaw's body just isn't here," Glen said. "But there is something kind of strange."

"What?" Nancy asked.

"Well, Sam Hughes, the night man at the morgue, remembered that his keys were missing for a while the other night. He couldn't find them the whole shift. Then just as he was about to leave—bingo—they were on the floor beneath the counter. Sam says he's positive they weren't there earlier. He looked."

"Thank you, Glen," Nancy said, excited. "You just solved one mystery for me!"

At lunchtime Nancy met Ned in the cafeteria. She told him about Glen's message. "I'm sure that's how the body snatcher got into the morgue. He lifted Sam's keys, made duplicates, then replaced them. He waited until the morgue was deserted, then let himself in and stole Dr. Shaw's body."

Ned bit into his hamburger. "But why?"

"Maybe an autopsy would reveal something he doesn't want known," Nancy guessed. Recalling her conversation with Trevor, she sighed. "I really feel bad for Trevor."

"So do I," admitted Ned.

"The only thing to do is wrap this investigation up as soon as possible and prove his innocence."

As they left the cafeteria a few minutes later, a familiar feminine voice sounded somewhere ahead of them in the corridor. Nancy looked up, listening. "Ned," she whispered. "I think that's Suzanne Welles."

Before Ned could respond, Suzanne sauntered around the corner. Gone was the serious woman of yesterday. She looked happy and bright.

To Nancy's amazement Trevor appeared right behind Suzanne. Before either Nancy or Ned could react, Suzanne slipped her arms around Trevor and planted a long kiss on his lips. And Trevor didn't fight back a bit!

Chapter

Nine

Ned murmured in Nancy's ear, "Talk about a lip lock."

Nancy was so surprised she didn't answer. Trevor finally surfaced from the kiss. When he saw Nancy and Ned, his face reddened. "Oh, hello. What are you two doing?" he asked, embarrassed.

"We just ate lunch," Nancy murmured.

The starry-eyed look on Suzanne's face made Nancy uneasy. What was going on? she wondered. The last she'd heard, Trevor didn't want Suzanne anywhere near him. But that kiss told a different story!

"Let's go, Trevor." Suzanne linked her arm through his. She seemed anxious to steer him away from Nancy and Ned. Trevor glanced back once, then disappeared around the corner.

"Now, what's that all about?" Ned wondered aloud, staring after them.

"I'm almost afraid to find out." Nancy made a face. "I didn't tell you before, but last night April said some pretty outrageous things about Trevor."

"You mean they're having a fight? What kind of things?"

"She thinks Trevor may have been responsible for her father's death after all. April's afraid he might have performed a mercy killing, because he knew how unhappy her father's illness was making her."

"What?" Ned's jaw dropped. "No way! Trevor would never do a thing like that. Not for any reason!" Nancy's continued silence prompted him to add, "You don't seriously believe her, do you?"

"No. But it is possible. Trevor admitted to me that Dr. Shaw asked him to end his suffering."

Ned stared at Nancy in shock. "And . . . ?"

"Trevor said he wouldn't even consider it," Nancy assured him. "A lot of people say things they don't mean when they're depressed."

"Like April herself?" Ned suggested, lifting a brow.

"Yes, like April. She's been under a lot of pressure too." Nancy shook her head. "I just can't seriously consider Trevor a suspect. He wouldn't take such a risk, even for April."

"If Trevor loves April," Ned said slowly, "why is he with Suzanne?"

"He was pretty upset when he found out what April had said to me. He might be with Suzanne because he's hurt." Another thought struck Nancy, and she felt cold inside. "Or maybe April's right, and he's with Suzanne because he's got a guilty conscience where April's concerned."

"Don't even think of it," said Ned, but the look on his face suggested he was worried, too. "I don't want to be around when April finds out about Trevor and Suzanne," he added quietly.

"Neither do I. Come on, let's get back to work."

They parted at the elevator. "I've got to race to the administration building," Ned said, holding her face between his palms and kissing her lightly. "Today's a late one. I won't be out until after six."

"Okay, that'll give me a few hours to do some detective work. I'll meet you in the lobby later."

* * *

The emergency room was a madhouse. An afternoon auto accident had the whole staff working frantically. Nancy raced around to help, filling out forms, directing patients into the examining rooms, and guiding them to the X-ray department whenever necessary.

While she worked, her mind kept turning over the riddle of this particular case. Who would want to ruin Trevor's career? Suzanne, for all her talk, was clearly still interested in Trevor. Would she have altered the files? *Could* she have? And now that Trevor seemed interested in Suzanne, would she change her tactics?

Then there was David Baines. He held a grudge against doctors in general and, it seemed, against the Shaws in particular. Nancy thought his bitterness might have something to do with having been expelled from medical school. And what had David meant by asking Dr. Rayburn about St. Louis?

The emergency room slowly cleared out. Nancy was surprised to see it was after four; she'd worked an hour overtime. Nancy finished up quickly and dashed for the door.

It was time to confront David Baines. He'd been underfoot during this whole investigation, needling April, talking to Dr. Rayburn. He'd even been on the cardiology floor just before Nancy had been attacked.

Thinking she might still catch him at the hospital, Nancy asked the switchboard operator to page him. The page went out over the loud-speaker, and Nancy waited over ten minutes, but Baines didn't show.

"He should be here," the receptionist informed Nancy. "His name's on the afternoon worksheet for the fifth floor."

"Thanks. I'll see if I can find him."

Nancy searched the fifth floor from end to end, going through the east and west wings several times. At the nurses' hub, she asked if anyone had seen him.

"Yeah, just a few minutes ago," a young R.N. answered. "He was called to Room five fifty-three."

Nancy hurried to Room 553. Peeking inside, she saw an elderly man napping in the hospital bed. There was no sign of David.

Back at the nurses' station, the same young nurse flagged her down. "He was just here! I told him a reddish blond candy striper was looking for him, and he said he'd find you."

Well, then, where is he? Nancy asked herself. She prowled the halls several more times, but

David Baines wasn't around. Could he be avoiding her?

Nancy punched the Up button on the elevator. When the doors slid open, however, she changed her mind, and took the stairs instead. She couldn't find David Baines on the seventh floor, but Dr. Rayburn might still be in his office. Of the two, Dr. Rayburn seemed more likely to tell Nancy what he and David had been discussing. Nancy rapped on the gray door to Rayburn's office. There was no answer, so Nancy let herself inside. Dr. Rayburn's secretary wasn't at her desk; apparently she'd gone home for the day.

This time the door to Dr. Rayburn's inner office was open a crack, and Nancy knocked again. "Dr. Rayburn?" she called, but without much hope. The door swung open wider. The room was empty, but a navy blue sports coat hung on the brass coatrack.

He must be coming back, Nancy thought, so she hovered in the doorway between Dr. Rayburn's inner office and his secretary's anteroom. To pass the time, she let her gaze travel over his medical diplomas and awards.

"Medical school in Boston," she murmured. "Well, that certainly doesn't have anything to do with Saint Louis." Maybe her theory about David Baines was all wet.

It was a quarter after six before Nancy gave up her vigil. She returned to the lobby, but there was no sign of Ned.

"Oh, Ms. Drew," the evening switchboard operator said, reading Nancy's name tag. "There's a message for you." She held out a pink slip.

Nancy took it from her hand and read: "Meet me at the administration building. Will be late. Ned."

Nancy walked down the corridor to the side exit door, pushed the bar, and stepped into the dusky evening air. The parking lot security lights were just flickering on.

The administration building was west of the hospital. Nancy walked along the sidewalk, then cut across the parking lot to save time. Her steps echoed on the pavement. She thought she heard the scrape of a sole behind her.

Glancing back, she let her gaze sweep the surrounding cars. A red Porsche was parked in the northwest corner of the lot. Baines's car!

Nancy hesitated, biting her lip. Ned, she decided, was going to have to wait. Turning, she hurried toward the gleaming red car. It was the latest style and year. "Must have cost him a fortune," she thought aloud.

Suddenly a gloved hand jerked Nancy off balance. Before she could yell, she felt a hand clamp over her mouth! Her arms were wrenched behind her back. Stunned, she immediately struggled, but her attacker was strong. He held her in a bone-crushing grip.

"Stay away from the hospital, Nancy Drew," a man's voice snarled viciously in her ear. "Unless you want to end up in the morgue!"

Chapter

Ten

NANCY KICKED BACK HARD, connecting with the man's left shin. Her attacker yelped with pain but kept dragging her toward the bushes near the dark corner of the parking lot.

Nancy twisted and fought, her heart pounding wildly. Her arms were held so tightly she couldn't free herself. The man was strong but slender. His voice sounded somewhat familiar. If only she could get a look at his face!

"Hey!" someone yelled from near the administration building.

At the same moment Nancy bit down on her

attacker's hand. "Help! Somebody help me!" she screamed when he let go of her mouth.

The sound of footsteps came pounding toward them. Her captor didn't wait. He threw her to the ground. Nancy hit the pavement and a loud groan escaped from her as the heels of her palms skidded against the asphalt. She scrambled almost instantly to her feet. Her attacker was zigzagging among the parked cars. Nancy ran after him, but by the time she got into gear, he was just a memory.

She stopped in the center of the lot, panting. Doubled over, she drew several long breaths, willing her heartbeat to slow down.

"Are you all right?" a voice asked.

"Yeah. Fine." She straightened up to see a worried-looking man in a lab coat standing beside her. "Thanks. He, uh, got away."

"You'd better come back inside the hospital and report this, miss. Have you still got your purse? This parking lot's getting dangerous!"

Nancy smiled an agreement. She let her would-be rescuer think this was just a random mugging, but she knew better.

Ned was pacing the hospital lobby when she returned. "Nancy! Where were you?" Seeing her torn dress and scraped palms, he asked, "What happened? Are you all right?"

"I'm fine," she assured him. "I was just on my way to the administration building to meet you when a guy attacked me from behind."

"What guy? What do you mean, the administration building? I got a message you were going to be late."

Nancy blinked. *"You* got a message *I* was going to be late?"

He nodded. "I picked it up here at the front desk."

Nancy turned to the two people at the desk. "Both messages were just dropped on the desk," the receptionist informed them when Nancy asked. "That's how it's done. People just pile them up and we route them to the right person or office."

"Someone wanted you to be outside alone," Ned said grimly to Nancy. "He meant to attack you!"

"I know," Nancy answered in a low voice, pulling Ned toward the door. When they were out of earshot of the others, she told him about her attacker's warning. "Ned, I'm not positive, but I think the guy who grabbed me was David Baines."

"Baines!"

"His voice was just a growl, but it sounded familiar. I got a look at him as he was running away. This guy had David's slender build and dark hair. It could have been someone else, I suppose, but I think it was David."

Ned's gaze narrowed. "Let's get out of here. We can pin Baines down tomorrow. I just want to get you home safe and sound."

Seeing that Ned was worried, Nancy agreed to wait until the next day to talk with Baines. They walked outside together in silence. Ned's car was parked near the largest dorm. As they approached it, Nancy stared ahead. Just visible far across the parking lot was a red Porsche.

"I'm sure that's David's car," Nancy said, pointing it out.

Before Ned could answer, they both noticed a brown-haired woman in a white lab coat as she walked down the sidewalk toward them, her head bowed. "Is that April?" Nancy asked Ned, peering through the gloom.

"If it is, we're saying hello. Then we're making tracks out of here. Agreed?"

"It *is* April," Nancy said, slipping from Ned's arms. "April!" she called, hailing her down.

April barely raised an arm. She walked over to Nancy and Ned in silence. There were tears glittering on her cheeks. She wiped at them and said in a trembling voice, "Trevor—is—with—*Suzanne!*"

Nancy appealed silently to Ned, who said softly, "April, I think Trevor's just reacting out of anger. He cornered Nancy this morning and wanted to know why you were so upset with him last night."

April stared at Nancy. "You told him what I said?" she gasped.

"I'm sorry—I had to," Nancy admitted. "I don't believe Trevor did anything wrong, but I have to consider every possibility."

"It doesn't matter." April sighed. "If he loved me, he wouldn't have gone back to Suzanne."

"I don't think he's really gone back to Suzanne," Nancy said.

"Oh, no?" April dug inside her purse for a tissue. "Then how do you explain the gold necklace Suzanne showed me when I ran into her in the cafeteria? It was a present from Trevor! That's a pretty expensive gift from someone who supposedly doesn't care about her!"

Nancy's lips parted in surprise. "Who told you Trevor gave it to Suzanne?"

"Suzanne did."

"Maybe she's lying. She struck me as the kind of person—"

"Thanks, Nancy. Really. But I don't want to talk about it. My father just died, and I'm still in shock. I can't take this, too." She drew a sharp breath through her teeth, exhaling it slowly. "I've asked the med school for a few days' release from classes, and they've given me a leave."

"What are you going to do?" Nancy asked, worried.

"I don't know. Maybe I'll leave town for a while. I need some time away to take care of my father's affairs and to put things in perspective. Thanks, Nancy, for all you've done." She managed a crooked smile and shook hands with Nancy and Ned. Then she walked into her dorm without a backward look.

"What do you make of that?" Ned asked as they headed to his car.

Nancy shook her head, climbing into the passenger seat. "It's a mess," she admitted.

They circled the hospital, and Nancy glanced toward the emergency room. A familiar figure was standing just inside the glass door, outlined against the light. "Ned!" Nancy cried excitedly. "Stop the car. That's David Baines! Now I'm sure he's the guy who grabbed me!"

Baines's hand was on the door, but he was talking to someone just out of sight.

"Ned, he's getting away!" Nancy cried as she leapt out of the car. David's silhouette was no longer visible. She ran to the emergency room, yanked open the door, and glanced both ways.

David was standing near the corner of the corridor, staring down the hall. There was a flurry of activity near the far end. Paramedics were bringing people in on stretchers. But the person David had been talking to was long gone.

"Is that the guy?" Ned asked, coming up behind Nancy.

Hearing him, David glanced back. His eyes widened when he saw Nancy hurrying toward him.

"I'd like to talk to you," Nancy began, but David was already moving toward the door.

"Yeah, well, I don't want to talk to you. I'm busy."

"Wait a minute, pal," Ned ordered, grabbing hold of the orderly's arm. David tried to pull free, but Ned's grip was too tight.

"Let go of me!" he demanded.

"In a minute," Ned said calmly. "Nancy has a few questions she'd like answered first."

"I don't have to talk to you! I'm calling security."

"Go right ahead," Nancy said coolly. "I'd like to speak to them, too. You see, someone attacked me a little while ago in the parking lot. I should report it."

David's eyes narrowed. "What's that got to do with me? I didn't do it."

His quick denial only strengthened Nancy's belief that David had indeed tried to drag her toward the bushes. But until she had real proof, she couldn't accuse him outright. "Didn't the nurse on five tell you I was looking for you earlier?" she asked him. "I get the feeling you've been trying to avoid me."

David glared at Ned's hand on his arm. "What do you two want?"

"Information," Nancy answered instantly. "I heard you were expelled from medical school in Saint Louis."

"So? I just got unlucky, okay? Since when is that a crime?" He sneered.

"Dr. Gerard Shaw was on staff at the medical school hospital in Saint Louis. And he was also consultant to the medical board of examiners."

"So?" David repeated. But his face drained of color. Bingo! Nancy thought with satisfaction.

"I don't have to listen to this!" David declared suddenly. He started struggling in earnest, and Ned practically had to pin his arms behind his back.

"You blamed Dr. Shaw for your being expelled," Nancy pressed. "That's right, isn't it?"

"Look, the old guy stuck his nose in where it

didn't belong. It had nothing to do with him! But those jerks at the hospital asked for his advice. They *listened* to him. And he didn't know anything about it!" With a supreme effort of will David jerked himself free and lunged for the door.

"Didn't know anything about what?" Nancy demanded, pushing open the door after David.

"Want me to tackle him?" Ned asked tersely.

"No, wait—"

Backing across the parking lot, David yelled, "You're way off base, girl detective! I didn't kill Dr. Shaw! But I know who did. And why!"

"Who?" Nancy asked, hurrying after him. "David, *who?*"

Headlights flashed at the edge of the parking lot. An engine revved. Nancy was so intent on David, she barely noticed. But David did. Slowly he turned his head, lights pinning him in their white glare.

"Nancy!" Ned called from behind her, panicked.

She glanced up. Roaring toward her and David was an ambulance! It screamed through the parking lot. Nancy dived to the right and rolled, her shoulder slamming into the curb.

She heard a shriek of terror. Glancing back,

she saw a flash of red and white. The ambulance was bearing down on David.

"David!" Nancy screamed.

To her horror, the ambulance hit David head on, tossing him like a rag doll up and over the hood. His limp body crumpled to the ground on the other side!

Chapter

Eleven

D AVID!" NANCY YELLED AGAIN.

She stumbled to her feet as Ned raced past her. The ambulance ripped by, careening around the corner, tires squealing.

David lay unconscious on the pavement. Nancy checked his breathing as Ned ran back to the hospital for help. She tore off her candy striper apron and wrapped it around him for warmth.

Within minutes a group of people had gathered around the scene and several paramedics appeared with a gurney. They lifted David carefully onto the gurney and wheeled him straight into the emergency room.

Ned touched Nancy's elbow. "This is a matter for the police. Whoever was driving that ambulance wasn't fooling around. He tried to kill David!"

Nancy nodded. "And David said Dr. Shaw was killed. That means we've got a murderer who's attempted to kill more than once."

"Including the attacks on you," Ned reminded her grimly.

Nancy nodded in response, wondering when the killer would take the opportunity to strike again.

Two hours later Nancy and Ned had explained everything to the chief of staff. Reluctantly, he called in the police. David was placed in intensive care and was still unconscious when Nancy and Ned were ready to leave.

"A concussion," Dr. Clemmons, the resident on duty, told them. "Possible ruptured spleen and a number of fractures."

"Will he be all right?" Nancy asked.

Clemmons was noncommittal. "His vital signs are stable."

Nancy and Ned walked back toward Ned's car. "It's kind of late for dinner," Nancy pointed out.

"Yeah." Ned sighed. "I've got some studying to do before I turn in."

"Should we forget about dinner?" Nancy suggested.

"Only if you promise to make it up to me." Ned kissed her, then grabbed her hand and steered her toward her own car.

"Promise," Nancy said.

He waited until she was safely behind the wheel and the doors were locked. Then he pointed at her and repeated, "Promise," in a voice that said there would be no backing out later.

The phone call woke Nancy from a deep, dreamless sleep. She opened one eye, checked her alarm clock, and groaned. "Go away," she told the ringing phone even as she groped to answer it.

"Is this Nancy Drew?" a young woman's voice asked.

"Yes, it is." Nancy yawned. It was only 5:30 A.M.

"Nancy, this is Emily Richards from the emergency room. I wanted to catch you before you left for the hospital. I realize this is short notice, but would you mind working from three o'clock to eleven today? Today's Friday, and we're always a lot busier in the afternoon and evenings on weekends. It would really help me out."

"Sure," she agreed, realizing she would have the entire morning to work on the case. "I'll see you this afternoon."

Nancy hung up the phone and yawned again, drawing her pillow over her head. She closed her eyes, but sleep eluded her. Who had tried to run David down the night before? How had the would-be murderer gotten hold of an ambulance? And did David really know who killed Dr. Shaw?

Flinging back the covers, Nancy climbed out of bed. She took a quick shower, dressed in faded jeans and an oversize cream-colored sweater, tied on her sneakers, and hurried downstairs.

Nancy called the River Heights police station and left a message for Detective John Ryan. They'd both been involved in a case Nancy called *Circle of Evil,* and even though they'd been working at cross-purposes, Detective Ryan had eventually admitted that Nancy was a talented investigator.

While she waited for some kind of answer, she did some thinking. The key to David Baines's involvement in this case had to be his expulsion from medical school. He'd turned completely white the night before when she brought the subject up. But did his grudge go deeper?

Nancy reached for the phone again. She dialed April's number at the dorm. The line rang so many times Nancy decided April must have left town, but April finally answered. "Hello?" she answered, her voice tired.

"Hi, April. It's Nancy. Sorry to bother you so early," Nancy apologized, "but I wondered if you could help me."

"Sure. How?"

"Did you hear what happened to David Baines last night?" April said no, and Nancy told her about the accident. April gasped, and Nancy said, "I need to find out more about David. I think he knows something."

"How can I help?"

"I need to know why he got expelled. Is there any way you can find out? Maybe from someone your father knew at the hospital in Saint Louis?"

"Well, Dr. Grafton's still there, I think," April said. "He's a friend of my father's. Or was." The line went quiet.

"April?" Nancy hated pushing her, but she really needed her help. "Would you mind calling Dr. Grafton and asking him about David?"

"I don't know what good it'll do, but I'll try."

"Thanks, April."

As soon as Nancy hung up, the phone rang. "Hello?" she asked into the receiver.

"Nancy Drew?"

She heard the smile in Detective Ryan's familiar voice. "Hi, there," she said. "As I recall, you once said you'd be happy to work with me on a case again."

"What kind of case?" he asked.

"Well, it's a little complicated. I need to do a background check on someone. His name is David Baines, and he's a patient in the hospital at Westmoor University Medical School. He works there, but last night—"

"He was mowed down by an ambulance. I've got the file right here, Nancy. Hospital security's guarding him against another attack. What specifically do you want to know?"

"Well, I'm working on a theory," she admitted. "I'd like to know about his bank balance."

"That's classified information," the detective warned.

"I know, but David seems to have a lot of unexplained money. He drives a Porsche, but he works as an orderly. Unless he has another job, I don't see how he can afford that kind of car."

Detective Ryan seemed to mull that over. "What do you think he's involved in?"

"When I know more, I'll tell all," Nancy countered, smiling to herself. Detective Ryan always tried to get her to reveal more than she was willing to tell him.

"Okay. Will you be home today?"

"I'll either be here or at the hospital." Nancy gave him the emergency room number.

"I'll call you," he promised.

The morning was passing quickly, so Nancy decided to get to the hospital. She changed into her candy striper outfit, grabbed her purse, and headed for the door. Just then the phone rang. Detective Ryan! Nancy made a mad dash for it.

"Nancy, is that you?" It was April.

"Right here. Have you got something for me?" she asked excitedly.

"Well, maybe. I'm not sure. I got in touch with Dr. Grafton."

"And?"

April hesitated. "Dr. Grafton wants this kept strictly confidential, but David was expelled for dangerous negligence. A patient died because David gave her the wrong medication. My father helped make the final decision to expel him."

"The wrong medication?" Nancy repeated, her pulse hammering. This was sounding increasingly familiar!

"The patient's husband threatened to sue the hospital. Nancy, Dr. Grafton told me something else, too. Dr. Rayburn worked at the same hospital. And he was one of the doctors who helped get David expelled!"

"Dr. Rex Rayburn? Chief cardiologist at W.U. Med School? *That* Dr. Rayburn?" Nancy asked, surprised.

"Small world, huh? Dr. Grafton says Dr. Rayburn was only there a short time."

"What was the name of the patient who died?" Nancy asked.

"Treadway. Anna Treadway," April answered. "She died of cardiac arrest. David took it upon himself to administer medicine to her even though he was just a student. She died as a result. The evidence was pretty clear."

Nancy whistled. A beep sounded in her ear. "April, I've got another call coming in. I'll talk to you later, okay? And thanks. Thanks a lot." Nancy touched the receiver, disconnecting April and connecting the incoming call. "Hello? Drew residence."

"Hi, there, Nancy," Detective Ryan's voice greeted her. "You were right on the money with Baines, so to speak. The guy's bank balance has a few extra zeros."

Nancy was elated. "How many extra zeros?"

"He's got thousands just sitting in a checking account. Now, where do you suppose that money came from, Detective Drew?"

"I'll let you know when I figure it out," Nancy said with a smile. "I owe you one."

"Since I'm being generous, here's one more item of interest: we found the ambulance that hit Baines. It was abandoned down by the river. No fingerprints. Officers are checking into how it was stolen. So far it looks as if someone just lifted the keys and took it."

Keys again. That someone must be fairly well connected to the hospital to be able to pull off a stunt like that, Nancy thought. She thanked the detective and hung up.

Nancy drove straight to the hospital, parked

near the emergency room door, and strode up the walkway. Running footsteps sounded behind her. Nancy whipped around, half expecting more danger. But it was Suzanne Welles coming across the parking lot.

"Nancy!" she cried, waving her arm. "I just saw you drive in. I've been looking for you all morning!"

"You have?"

"Yes." Suzanne slowed down, her fingers lightly touching the gold necklace encircling her neck.

"That's beautiful," Nancy remarked, eyeing the necklace.

"Trevor gave it to me," she answered proudly, as if she'd been waiting for Nancy to bring up the subject. "Nancy, I've been thinking about what you said the other day. About someone setting up Trevor. That's why Dr. Shaw's body is missing, isn't it? Whoever stole it must know an autopsy would show that Trevor is innocent."

Nancy regarded her silently, waiting for her to get to the point.

Suzanne hesitated. "I have an idea who the body snatcher might be."

"You do?"

She nodded. "April Shaw."

"April!" Nancy was taken aback.

"I know on the surface it doesn't seem possible, but think about it," Suzanne went on hurriedly, before Nancy could respond. "She could have killed her father. She hated watching him suffer. She as much as said she couldn't wait until his suffering was over. And now I'm convinced that she only pretended to love Trevor!"

"Suzanne," Nancy protested.

"She used him," Suzanne went on, her jaw tightening angrily. "She needed someone to throw the blame on, and she used Trevor. Have you seen April cry any real tears over her father's death? No! Nancy Drew, if you're looking for a murderer, look no further than April Shaw!"

Chapter

Twelve

O H, COME ON, SUZANNE," Nancy said. "April loves Trevor. They've been engaged for months, since long before Dr. Shaw came to visit her."

Suzanne lifted her chin. "I notice you don't deny that she could have been involved in a mercy killing."

"I only agree that she wanted her father's suffering to end. That's a long way from murder."

"Not that long."

They were at a stalemate. Nancy looked into Suzanne's dark eyes, wondering if her accusations had any basis in truth. A tiny seed of doubt

grew inside her. April was an emotional wreck—
of that much Nancy was certain. April had been
very composed after her father's death—
unnaturally so, Nancy had thought at the time.
Could her emotional state now be caused by
guilt?

Nancy left Suzanne and went into the hospital.
It was almost two. Shaking her head clear of
Suzanne's allegations, Nancy used the lobby pay
phone to call April. "Hi, April. It's Nancy. I've
been thinking about a few things and wondered if
you could help me again. I'd like to know more
about what happened to Anna Treadway in Saint
Louis. Is there any way I could get my hands on
some old records? I have a hunch that what's
happening now must relate somehow to that
tragedy."

"I could call Dr. Grafton again," April said
doubtfully. "He might be willing to let you see
the files."

"Tell him about what happened to David. We
don't want any more 'accidents.'"

"Okay, Nancy."

Nancy hung up, lost in thought. She gasped
when a hand suddenly grabbed her arm.
"Trevor!" she exclaimed, whipping around.

"Sorry to frighten you. I couldn't help overhearing. You were talking to April, weren't you?"

His handsome face was set and serious. Nancy could no more read his mind than she could Suzanne's. "Yes, I was."

A muscle in his jaw flexed. "How is she?"

"Okay, I guess. She's trying to put the last few days in perspective. They've really taken an emotional toll." When Trevor didn't respond, Nancy added lightly, "I saw the necklace you gave Suzanne. It's beautiful."

"The gold necklace?" Trevor asked blankly. "Suzanne showed it to you?"

Nancy nodded. "And she showed it to April, too."

"What! But I gave that necklace to Suzanne years ago. It was a birthday gift." He looked stunned. "You don't think April believes I gave it to Suzanne recently!"

"As a matter of fact, that's exactly what she thinks," Nancy replied, deciding to use the opportunity to clear up some facts. "Trevor, what's going on between you and Suzanne? Could you be using her to get back at April?"

Trevor opened his mouth, then clamped it shut. He strode away without answering. Nancy realized she didn't have time to follow him. It was time to show up at the emergency room.

The afternoon passed quickly; as the head nurse had said, Fridays were really busy. Ned appeared at five o'clock, ready to leave. "The week's seminar is over," he said, smiling. "Now I've got to decide if this is the kind of work I want to do. You know, I really should take you on a tour of some of the labs and classrooms before we leave. All you've seen is the hospital. This place is huge. I even got to see one of the refrigerators where they keep organs for transplants."

Nancy made a face. "I think I'll pass on that. Besides, I have seen more than the hospital. I've been to the administration building."

"I wish you were off duty," Ned said wistfully. "You could make good on our dinner date."

"Too bad I'm stuck here until eleven," Nancy said, disappointed.

A voice laughed behind her and Nancy turned to see Emily Richards. "You can go if you want," she said, smiling. "It was really unfair of me to ask you to change your schedule. You're not even employed here."

"But I thought you were shorthanded."

"We are, but it's really nurses we need. I've managed to find some who want to earn overtime pay. Don't worry, Nancy. I've got enough candy stripers. Go enjoy yourself."

"So where do you want to eat?" Ned asked, once he and Nancy were in the corridor outside the emergency room.

Nancy untied her candy striper apron and pulled it over her head. "Ned, I know you've heard this before, but I'd like to stay at the hospital a little longer. I want to try to see David. He's our strongest link in this case."

Ned considered. "Well, okay. As long as you make it up to me later."

She smiled. "Maybe over dinner we can brainstorm about where Dr. Shaw's body could be."

Nancy and Ned headed for the third floor. It wasn't hard to find David's room. A gray-suited security guard stood outside the door, his beefy arms folded across his chest. Just looking at him made Nancy's hopes sink. He didn't seem the type to bend the rules even a little.

Nancy hovered at the corridor juncture, turning her back on the guard so he wouldn't get a good look at her.

"What do you want to do?" Ned whispered in her ear.

"I don't know, but I've got to get in there somehow. If only I were a doctor, or something," Nancy murmured, thinking aloud.

"Well . . ." A gleam of mischief entered Ned's eyes. "You *can* be a doctor for a while. At least you can fool people into thinking you are."

"How?"

Ned led her toward the elevator. "Follow me."

He guided her to a locker room next to the operating rooms. "Check out the lockers," he told her. "Some aren't locked. On our tour I noticed some of the doctors left their lab coats hanging up."

"Ned, you're wonderful!" Nancy cried, pushing open the door.

The fourth locker produced results. Inside was a white lab coat with a lapel pin attached. Nancy slipped it on and met Ned in the outer hall.

"Dr. Marcia Smythe," Ned read, when she rejoined him in the hall.

A pair of glasses were nestled in the coat pocket, and Nancy stuck them on her nose after she pulled her hair back. "Do I look old enough?" she asked anxiously.

"Not really. But the hair and the glasses help." They headed back to floor three. "I'll keep a lookout at the corner of the corridor in case you get in," said Ned. "If anyone comes, I'll create some kind of distraction to give you time to get out."

"Wish me luck," Nancy murmured, straightening her shoulders.

"Luck," Ned said softly. "And be careful."

Nancy strode purposefully down the hall, glancing around. Two doors down from David's room, a gurney covered with a sheet was waiting outside an open door. The rest of the doors were closed. Only she and the security guard were in the corridor.

Nancy's heart was pounding in double time, but she hid her nervousness behind a tight smile. "If you'll excuse me," she said, pulling open the door to David's room with authority. She looked carefully at the guard. Would her disguise work?

The security man simply nodded and let her pass. With a silent sigh of relief, Nancy let herself into the room. She slipped the glasses back into the coat pocket.

The room was dimly lit. Light from the outside parking lamps filtered in through the blinds. David lay on the far bed, a bandage around his head, one side of his face bruised and scraped. He was tossing restlessly under the covers.

"David," Nancy whispered, glancing nervously over her shoulder to the door. "Can you hear me?"

"Doctor . . . Rayburn . . ." he muttered.

"No, it's Nancy Drew," she said swiftly, touching his arm. "You were talking to me outside the emergency room last night. Do you remember?"

His eyelids fluttered open. He seemed to focus on her. "The ambulance," he mumbled.

Nancy nodded encouragingly.

David licked his lips. "It was in Saint Louis . . . She was dead. . . ."

"Anna Treadway?" Nancy asked quickly.

A small sound escaped David's throat. "Not my fault. Not my fault—it was an accident—Dr. Shaw . . ."

"How did it happen?" Nancy asked. "How did the accident happen?"

David sighed deeply and seemed to sink into a deeper sleep. His breathing became slow and regular. His eyelids closed.

"David?" Nancy whispered. "David?" Outside the door she heard cushioned footsteps coming down the hall. Anxiously she searched for a place to hide. But the guard already knew she was in the room!

Nancy heard Ned's voice outside, speaking loudly. "Hey, I'm lost. Can you tell me where ICU is?"

Nancy's heart nearly stopped. He was warning her!

Gathering all her courage, Nancy swung open the door and strode into the hall as if she owned the place. A nurse was standing next to Ned, holding a tray of small white paper cups. The patients' evening medicine. She glanced up at Nancy, her brows raised as she brushed past and entered Baines's room.

The gurney Nancy had spied in the hallway was now standing just inside a room with an open door. Nancy glanced back at Ned. To her dismay she saw Dr. Clemmons just rounding the corner! She had to get out of sight before her cover was blown!

Nancy's eyes darted wildly in all directions. Nowhere to hide. Turning into the open room, Nancy stopped short. An orderly was making up one of the beds. A patient lay on the other bed, asleep. Nancy pressed herself against the wall, heart thudding. Where could she hide?

The gurney.

Without another thought, she lay on the gurney and pulled the sheet over her head.

"You're Nancy Drew's friend, aren't you?" she heard Dr. Clemmons demand loudly.

"That's right," Ned answered.

"Well, where is she? You were with her a little while ago."

"She's not here."

"Who do you mean?" the security guard asked.

Nancy's heart sank. Here it comes.

"I mean a red-haired girl who doesn't know how to obey hospital rules," Dr. Clemmons said angrily. "We're talking about a patient's life! If I find she's inside this room, I'll make certain she's removed from this hospital!"

Nancy drew a quiet, shallow breath. Seconds later, she nearly jumped when Ned whispered near her ear, "Nancy?"

"Can I help you?" The orderly who had been tidying up the room asked.

Nancy froze.

"I, uh, was just looking for a friend," said Ned.

"No one here." The gurney suddenly lurched away from the wall. Nancy had to fight back a gasp. To her horror, she realized the orderly was pushing her out of the room! "Excuse me, I have to take this body down to the morgue."

The morgue?

"Er, *this* body?" Nancy heard Ned ask.

"Yeah, buddy. You got a problem with that?"

Nancy nearly choked as the gurney was pushed from the semidark room to the brightly lit hallway. The wheels clattered and squeaked as she felt herself being pushed in the direction of David's room!

"A red-haired girl?" the guard was repeating thoughtfully. "Reddish blond hair?"

"Is she in there?" Clemmons demanded. Nancy heard a flurry of footsteps. Grimacing, she realized Clemmons wasn't going to wait for an answer. He was heading straight into David's room.

There were more footsteps. The gurney stopped short. Nancy realized the jig was up.

"All right, Ms. Drew." Dr. Clemmons's voice boomed with suppressed anger. "You're coming with me! The chief of staff won't appreciate your having gone against direct orders!"

Chapter

Thirteen

NANCY COUNTED her heartbeats and waited for Clemmons to yank the sheet back.

"What are you doing, Dr. Clemmons?" a female voice asked.

The nurse! Nancy realized with relief. That's who Clemmons was addressing, thinking she was Nancy!

"I—I—" Clemmons sputtered, confused.

The gurney lurched into motion again. Nancy felt herself being wheeled away from David's room. She had to hold back her laughter as she heard Clemmons's embarrassed apology.

"Hey!" Ned called, his footsteps falling into step beside the orderly's.

"Get lost, buddy," the orderly growled impatiently. "Go make a nuisance of yourself somewhere else."

Nancy was thinking fast. When she felt the wheels turn the corner, she threw off the sheet. The orderly, a young man with red hair, shrieked.

"Miraculous recovery," Ned said with a grin, grabbing Nancy's arm.

They dashed down the hall to the stairway and took the stairs at a run. Halfway to the first floor Nancy collapsed in a fit of laughter. "Did you see the orderly's face?"

"Yeah." Ned grinned. "But you should have seen Clemmons's face when that nurse walked out of David's room! He turned bright red. Did you get a chance to talk to David?"

"No, but he was mumbling in his sleep. He brought up Saint Louis again. The key to the mystery's got to be what happened to Anna Treadway."

Ned thought for a moment. "Do you suppose David moved Dr. Shaw's body to cover up the fact that he'd killed him? He could have stolen Sam's keys and removed the body."

"That means he killed Shaw for revenge, but it

doesn't explain where the body is now. And it doesn't explain who was driving the ambulance that ran David down."

"Who else do you think could be involved in this Saint Louis business?" Ned asked.

Nancy reflected for a moment. "Well, maybe Dr. Rayburn. David did say something to him about Saint Louis outside his office, and April said Rayburn worked at the same hospital. He might have a grudge against David, too."

"It'd have to be a pretty serious grudge to give him a motive for killing them," Ned reasoned.

Ned was probably right. "What about someone connected with Anna Treadway?" Nancy suggested, looking for an alternative. "I mean, she was killed. Maybe one of her relatives blamed David and Dr. Shaw for her death. April told me Treadway's husband threatened to file a malpractice suit."

"Well, whoever's behind all these incidents is in pretty tight with this hospital. Could one of Anna Treadway's relatives be employed here?" he asked.

"I'll check it out." Nancy frowned; she felt very frustrated. "But why would one of her relatives want to frame Trevor? It keeps coming back to that. And why involve the hospital at all? If someone wanted to get rid of David or Dr. Shaw, there are a lot easier ways to do it than at the hospital." Ned opened the door to the first floor as Nancy continued. "I need more information about what happened to Anna Treadway. I'm going to call Detective Ryan to see if he can help me."

Nancy was heading for a pay phone when Trevor walked into the first floor lobby. He seemed a little embarrassed at seeing them. "Seminar's over, right?" he said to Ned, not knowing what else to say. "So how did you like it?"

"Okay, I guess. Although I'm glad it's you in the anatomy lab, not me."

"Detective Ryan's not in this evening," a female voice told Nancy. "Can someone help you?"

But Nancy wasn't listening. Her thoughts were buzzing. Anatomy lab! she thought excitedly. Dr. Shaw's body wasn't in the morgue, but it had to be hidden in a cold place! "Uh, thanks, no," she managed to say into the phone before hanging up.

"Nancy, I need to talk to you," Trevor said, sighing. "I've been such a jerk. I shouldn't have kissed Suzanne," Trevor went on. "You were right. I was just mad. I mean, how could April think I killed her father! I'm a doctor, for crying out loud. I would never do anything like that."

"April's just upset," Ned said.

Realizing they were both looking at her, Nancy surfaced. "Do you think April could have performed a mercy killing herself?" Nancy asked Trevor.

He looked incredulous. "No way!"

"Suzanne thought she might be capable of it."

Trevor's eyes sparked with fury. "I'm beginning to see Suzanne would do anything to hurt April. What an idiot I've been!"

"You're sure April's innocent?" Nancy asked.

"Absolutely." Trevor's face was serious. "April loved her father. She hated to see him suffer, but she would never have ended his life. She cared for him too much."

Trevor's words rang with sincerity. Nancy smiled. "I believe you," she admitted. "I never really took Suzanne's accusations seriously, but I wanted to hear how you felt. What about Suzanne? Could she have murdered Dr. Shaw? As a way of putting the blame on you?"

"That's reaching even farther. Suzanne would never jeopardize her career that way. Her work is too important to her. A lot more important than *I* ever was," Trevor added.

"So who did it?" Ned asked.

"I'm not sure," Nancy said slowly, "but I think I know where to find Dr. Shaw's body."

"I can almost hear the gears turning in your

head," Ned said, grinning. "Out with it, Ms. Drew."

"You're the one who keeps talking about the anatomy lab." Nancy laughed. "Isn't there a dissecting lab in the classroom building? And doesn't the medical school use cadavers in anatomy class?"

"Well, yes," Trevor answered. "But we only work on authorized bodies."

"But an unauthorized body could be hidden among the cadavers, couldn't it? Isn't there some kind of cold storage place where cadavers are kept?"

"Well, sure, there's a freezer, but—"

"That's right!" Ned snapped his fingers. "A huge walk-in freezer. The classroom building used to be the old hospital. The freezer there is right next to the dissecting lab!"

"There are cadavers in the freezer," Trevor admitted. "But I'm sure it's been searched."

"The search has really only taken place at the hospital," Nancy reminded him. "And it would be a simple matter to change the name on a body. No one would be the wiser."

Trevor nodded, blinking rapidly. "That's true," he said with dawning amazement. "Nancy, you're right! Listen, I'm still on duty, and I've got to check on one more patient before I take a break. Give me a few minutes and I'll meet you at the freezer."

"Ned and I'll wait for you there," said Nancy. "We'll need you to identify Dr. Shaw's body."

Trevor nodded. "Okay. I'll be there in about twenty minutes, maybe a little longer if I run into a snag or two. I can't afford to mess up on my duties right now, or I'll be suspended." He turned, then hesitated, glancing back. "Want me to call security?"

"Let's wait to see if my theory pans out," Nancy suggested.

"Right." Trevor tried to smile.

Nancy and Ned hurried to the nearest exit. Ned guided her across the campus to the classroom building, which housed the anatomy lab. It was in the oldest section of the school, an ivy-clad brick building with poor lighting. Just thinking about the task in front of them had Nancy looking over her shoulder.

"Think we're being followed?" Ned asked, glancing around suspiciously.

"I don't know. This building's a little creepy. Didn't you say something about tunnels under it?"

"Yeah, they run from here to the hospital. It's a great way to move bodies without upsetting visitors."

"That's how our body snatcher did it, then,"

Nancy declared. "He must have moved the body through a tunnel from the hospital to the anatomy lab. Which floor is the lab on?"

"Third. I checked after April quizzed me the other day."

They hurried upstairs. Nancy caught the smell of formaldehyde as soon as they pushed open the door to the third floor.

"It's right down here," said Ned, indicating a door with Anatomy written across its pebbled glass window.

"It's locked," Nancy said, trying the handle.

"Should we just wait outside?"

Nancy nodded, and they stood quietly outside the door. Nancy's thoughts were on David Baines. "David could have moved the body," she muttered. "Maybe he murdered Dr. Shaw and was afraid the autopsy would prove it."

A slight noise from inside the anatomy lab interrupted Nancy's thoughts.

"What was that?" Ned asked softly.

"Someone's in there!" Nancy whispered. She quickly pulled her lock-picking kit from her purse and quietly worked the lock with a slim metal tool. The tiny clicks she made sounded to her like pistol shots in the dead quiet of the hall.

Seconds later the knob turned noiselessly in her hand. Pressing a finger to her lips, she squeezed inside the room. Row upon row of tables filled the enormous classroom. A thin light glowed beneath a far door.

Ned's hand clamped down on her shoulder. "Stay here," he mouthed to her. Nancy vehemently shook her head, but Ned ignored her. His running shoes made no noise as he crept across the linoleum floor. Nancy had little choice but to watch him steal toward the far door. Someone needed to stand guard.

At the end of the room, Ned touched a finger to the door. It swung in, unlatched. He gave Nancy the thumbs-up sign, then disappeared inside.

Nancy chewed on her lower lip. Minutes dragged by. She stole a glance at her watch every thirty seconds. Where was Trevor? Why hadn't Ned returned?

At the end of fifteen minutes Nancy couldn't stand it any longer. She left her post and tiptoed hurriedly to the door Ned had pushed open. Another classroom lay beyond, lit by a row of ceiling lights. Nancy's heartbeat quickened as she moved forward.

She cautiously glanced around that classroom's door frame. A giant metal door stood at the end of a short hallway. The freezer! Nancy moved toward it and pulled back the latch. It clicked loudly and the door creaked open.

With a glance inside Nancy knew she had found the place where the cadavers were kept.

Thick translucent plastic sacks hung from hooks. But Nancy barely noticed. Because directly in her line of vision lay Ned, sprawled on the cold wooden floor. And a pair of hands covered by surgical gloves were pushing his limp body inside a huge plastic sack!

Chapter

Fourteen

N ED!" NANCY SCREAMED, racing forward.

The hands jerked back. Then Nancy heard a clatter and running footsteps. She reached Ned as a man dressed in surgical greens slipped behind a tall stack of boxes.

Nancy checked Ned for a pulse and realized he was breathing steadily. Then, quick as a cat, she leapt to her feet and began to chase the assailant. The huge freezer was filled with stacks of hospital supplies. Nancy spotted her quarry at the end of a long row of boxes. "Stop!" she yelled.

The intruder half turned toward her. Nancy charged forward. Now there were barely ten feet between them. In a flash, Nancy grabbed his sleeve before he could slip away. She held his right arm, trying to see his face. His mouth and nose were covered by a surgical mask and he wouldn't turn her way.

"Nancy!" Trevor's voice called from the other end of the freezer.

"Over here!" she yelled. At that moment, the man jammed his left elbow into her stomach, knocking the wind from her. He threw her down and zigzagged through the rows of boxes back toward Trevor!

"Trevor," Nancy called weakly, trying to warn him.

Racing footsteps echoed through the refrigerator. Boxes crashed to the floor.

"What the—" Trevor said, but his words were cut off. Nancy heard a groan; then the footsteps receded through the classrooms. She heard the click of a latch.

The door! Nancy thought with fear, staggering to her feet. All three of them were locked inside the freezer!

She hurried toward Trevor, cold air flooding into her lungs. When Nancy found him, Trevor lay in a heap. Luckily there was a latch on the inside of the door. It turned easily in Nancy's hand, and she breathed a sigh of relief as the door opened. Far ahead Nancy heard the intruder's footsteps disappearing. She propped open the door with a box.

"Trevor, are you all right?" Nancy asked anxiously, gently slapping his face.

Trevor shook his head and sat up, looking around dazedly. "Did you see him? He slammed into me before I got a chance to do anything."

"I didn't see his face. Come on, we've got to help Ned."

Trevor followed after Nancy. Ned still lay unconscious on the floor. Trevor bent over him. "His eyelids are fluttering. That's a good sign. Quick, help me carry him out of here. We've got to warm him up. Be careful with his neck. I'll take his shoulders; you take his feet."

Nancy was glad Trevor was there. He immediately got down to business. By the time they carried Ned to the warm classroom, he had begun to come around. "Nancy," he mumbled.

"Shhh," she said.

"Lay him down here," Trevor said, settling Ned on the floor. He yanked a penlight out of his coat pocket and examined Ned's eyes. "You look all right, my friend," he said seriously, running expert fingers around Ned's head. Ned winced. "But you've got a nasty bump at the base of your skull."

"Where'd he go?" Ned demanded, trying to sit up.

"He's long gone," Nancy said. "Are you okay?"

"You'd better get over to the hospital and have a thorough examination," Trevor told him.

Against his protests, Trevor and Nancy helped Ned toward the door. He assured them he could walk on his own, but Trevor was reluctant to let him make the trek by himself.

"What do you want to do?" Trevor asked Nancy.

"Get Ned to an examining room, then find Dr. Shaw's body."

"You guys go and look for the body," Ned ordered, leaning against the doorjamb. "I'll be okay."

Trevor glanced at him. "I could make a quick check and meet you both at the hospital."

"I don't want to leave you here alone, Trevor," Nancy said, worried.

"Go, Trevor," Ned insisted. "I can wait."

"Okay, I'll be right back." Trevor went back inside the freezer. Nancy waited with Ned, glad to see color slowly return to his cheeks.

"Stop looking at me as if I'm an invalid. I'm fine, I tell you. Who was that guy? All I saw was a green mask."

"Well, it wasn't David Baines, but it was a man. Our mysterious Mr. X. I'll bet he's the same person who ran David down in the ambulance.

And I'll bet David was blackmailing him—that would explain David's hefty bank balance."

"Blackmailing him for what?"

Nancy shook her head. "I don't know. If it has to do with Anna Treadway, then it's got to be someone who—" Nancy sucked in a breath. "Oh, I've been so blind! Ned, I think I know who's behind this!"

"Who?" Ned asked, just as Trevor came striding toward them.

"It's there!" Trevor said excitedly. "Dr. Shaw's body is there under another name. I recognized it because the name on the body was that of a patient who died here months ago. There's no way they'd still have the cadaver."

"I think our mysterious Mr. X was trying to move the body," Nancy said.

"Then we've got to call security," Trevor said. "There's a phone at the end of the hall. I'll stay here while you make the call. When the security guards get here, I'll tell them to take Dr. Shaw's body to the pathology lab in the basement of the hospital building. You take Ned to the emergency room. I'll meet you there later."

"I tell you I'm fine!" Ned said again, but Nancy steered him out of the room.

Just as they were disappearing into the hallway, Trevor called out, "Would you phone April? Let her know her father's body's been found."

"Sure," Nancy yelled back. Spying a telephone in the hallway, she and Ned quickened their steps.

"Okay, Nancy, spill it," Ned said. "Who do you think stole Dr. Shaw's body?"

She grinned. "How does Dr. Rayburn grab you?"

"Rayburn! Why Rayburn?"

They had reached the phone, so Nancy shook her head and dialed the reception hub. She asked for several security guards to be sent to the anatomy lab at Dr. Trevor Callahan's request. Ned waited impatiently for her to finish.

"All right, give," he said when they reached the first floor and headed back across the gloomy campus to the hospital.

"Rayburn was a doctor at the Saint Louis medical school. He was also partially responsible for David getting expelled."

"But what has that got to do with killing Dr. Shaw?"

"I'm not sure—yet. After all, Shaw and Rayburn were on the same side. But I think Rayburn's the connection. He knows something. Maybe something he wants buried."

"What are you going to do now?"

"Go to Rayburn's office," Nancy said determinedly as they walked into the emergency room. "There's something I have to check out."

"I'm coming with you."

"No way." She half pushed him down the hallway. "This man needs a doctor," she said, as one of the emergency room nurses looked up inquiringly. "I'll be back," she whispered to Ned as another candy striper came toward him with a warm smile on her face and a clipboard in hand.

Trapped, Ned muttered, "Traitor," out of the side of his mouth.

Nancy headed straight for Dr. Rayburn's office. When she found the door locked, she wasn't surprised. With her lock pick, Nancy let herself into the secretary's front office and then into Rayburn's inner office.

Inside, the blinds were drawn, but she didn't dare turn on a light. Instead she pulled her penlight from her purse and flicked on the small beam of light.

Rayburn's mahogany desk was an antique. Rows of locked drawers ran along the front. Nancy painstakingly jimmied the lock on each one and searched quickly through the sheaves of paper within. Finally she unlocked a slim drawer near the top and found a medical file inside it. She placed the folder on the smooth desktop and began thumbing through the papers. Nothing.

She was replacing the file when she noticed that the back of the drawer moved slightly. Pushing against the wooden slat, she realized it was a drawer divider. Elated, she removed the slat and found another file behind it. When she opened it, a single piece of paper fluttered onto the desktop.

It was a typewritten demand for ten thousand dollars, and a threat. The words jumped out at her.

Pay by Thursday unless you want to face a very messy malpractice suit. You know who I mean. I've got a Porsche to pay for, remember?

The note was unsigned, but Nancy knew it must have been from David Baines. Blackmail! she realized excitedly. That explained David's fat bank balance. But Rayburn involved in a malpractice suit? What *did* David have on the man?

Nancy quickly replaced the file and relocked the drawer. She sat for a moment in utter silence, thinking hard. Through the blinds, the outdoor security lights glinted in streaks on Dr. Rayburn's framed certificates. With sudden insight, Nancy jumped to her feet and ran the beam of her flashlight over Dr. Rayburn's Boston medical diploma.

"So that's it!" she murmured, focusing on Dr. Rayburn's printed name.

Nancy quickly closed the door to Rayburn's

office behind her, crept through the secretary's room to check the hall, then slipped into the hallway and softly locked the outer door behind her. Now she had all the facts!

She was on her way back to the emergency room to meet Ned and Trevor when she thought about Dr. Shaw's body. She hurried to the elevator and punched the button for the basement. Once she made certain that Dr. Shaw's body had been moved and was now secure and safe in the pathology lab, she could rejoin Ned.

The basement was deserted. The overhead fluorescent lights buzzed faintly as she walked down the corridor. Nancy's heartbeat fluttered. Her every nerve was on edge.

The door to the pathology lab was standing wide open. As Nancy glanced inside, her heart jumped to her throat. Slumped on the floor were the bodies of two security guards—the guards who had just brought the body here! She rushed forward, stunned, then stooped to check their pulses. They were alive, but out cold.

Through another door she saw a man in a white coat sprawled across a counter. Nancy ran forward. He, too, was breathing but unconscious. His sleeves were rolled up, and she could see a small red mark on his forearm. So that was how the intruder had knocked them out so easily. They'd been jabbed with a hypodermic needle!

Hearing a familiar squeaking, Nancy spun around in time to see a draped gurney being pulled through a low door at the far end of the room. Nancy raced toward it. Ahead was a long narrow hallway. The tunnel, she realized. Dr. Shaw's body was being stolen again!

Chapter

Fifteen

STOP!" NANCY SCREAMED. "Stop!"

A man in green surgical gear glanced backward. The same man who had attacked her in the anatomy lab! Nancy caught a glimpse of familiar scowling black eyebrows just as he thrust the gurney toward her with a mighty shove.

Nancy dodged, but the gurney hit her hip, knocking her against the wall. The sheet slipped to reveal a body. It must be Shaw. Her quarry took off at a run. Without further hesitation Nancy raced after him into the old tunnel.

The ceiling grew lower. The floor sloped down

beneath her feet. The lighting was weak and shadowy. As she progressed farther, the tunnel grew narrower and less well tended. Though the walls and floor were concrete, Nancy could smell the faint dank scent of earth. She wished she'd told Ned and Trevor she was going to the pathology lab. She could use a little backup.

She was certain now that she was following Dr. Rayburn. Should she just give up and go for help? Though the eerie tunnel made her a little nervous, she wasn't willing to turn back. Who knew what Rayburn would do next? She had to stop him.

As a precaution, she tore off some of the hem from her lab coat. She tied a thin strip to one of the metal light protectors and pinned Dr. Marcia Smythe's nametag on it. If Ned came down this tunnel, he'd know she'd been here.

Thirty feet later, the tunnel forked in two. Nancy paused. Kneeling down, she pressed her ear to the cold concrete. Faintly, down the tunnel to her right, she heard the impact of hurried footfalls. She tore off another strip from the coat, marking the passage.

Nancy picked up her pace. If Rayburn reached the end of the tunnel before she did, she might never find him. He obviously knew these tunnels and buildings intimately.

Straight ahead of her, a wooden door blocked her exit. She strained but was able to pull it open. To one side, a flight of stairs led up. Her sense of direction told her she was beneath the medical classroom building.

Climbing the stairs, Nancy reached a landing and another door. It was warmer here. She cracked the door open and saw she was in an unfamiliar basement with huge, dusty insulated pipes running beneath the ceiling.

Nancy stepped forward cautiously. She heard a sound behind her. She whipped around in time to see those same dark eyebrows and steely eyes. Hands clamped around her arms, but Nancy was quick. She twisted free, snatching off the man's mask.

"Dr. Rex Rayburn," she said coolly. "How come I'm not surprised?"

"Because you're too diligent for your own good," he said. "Sorry, Ms. Drew."

Rayburn grabbed her, and a second later she felt the prick of a needle. Panicking, Nancy struggled free of his grasp. "But you underestimated me. I've got too much to lose. You must understand."

Nancy glanced in horror at the tiny puncture mark on her arm.

"Just a sedative," he told her. "Until I can

come up with a better plan. I must admit, you really caught me off guard." His expression was more concerned than angry. "I really wish things could be different, but I'm afraid you know too much."

Nancy opened her mouth, hoping to try to reason with him, but her tongue suddenly felt thick and woolly. Dr. Rayburn's face dissolved into a watery pool.

She felt his hands catch her as she crumpled to the floor.

The light hurt Nancy's eyes. She squeezed them shut and turned her head. She raised an arm, only to have it fall back limply.

Memory returned in a cold rush. Dr. Rayburn!

She forced her eyes open. She was lying on some kind of table in a room with cinder-block walls painted a dull beige. Her head ached. Squinting, she saw there was a bright lamp directly above her.

She was lying on an operating table!

A tinkling noise caught her attention. She turned her head in the direction of the sound. Dr. Rayburn was busying himself at a stainless-steel portable table.

Nancy's heart lurched. What was he planning?

It took all her energy and willpower to force

her limbs to move. Fighting back a groan, she rolled onto the floor. Her legs were jelly.

"Oh, no, Ms. Drew." Rayburn was beside her in two quick steps, grabbing her arm and helping her to her feet. "You can't leave."

"Where am I?" Nancy's tongue slurred.

"This is the operating room beneath the medical classroom building. It isn't used much anymore except by students, and generally they don't work on live subjects. But every once in a while . . ."

Dr. Rayburn put her back on the table. This time he strapped her down, making certain her hands and feet were securely restrained. "The facilities are still quite good," he went on, "if a bit isolated."

She saw him connect the tubes that were hanging from the wall into a machine near her head. He flicked a switch, and there was a faint hissing sound. Then he turned back to the table, snapping on a pair of plastic gloves. Nancy's head was clearing. She twisted against the leather bands. "People know where I am. You'll never get away with this!"

"Oh, yes. I'm afraid I will." One hand reached for the gas mask attached to the machine.

Anesthesia! Nancy realized in horror.

"I truly am sorry," he said again, advancing on

her with the mask. In his other hand he held a deadly sharp scalpel!

Nancy's terrified gaze fell on the surgical knife. It glinted menacingly in the intense light, poised above her head. In another second Dr. Rayburn was going to operate. On her!

Chapter

Sixteen

NANCY THOUGHT QUICKLY. Her only chance of survival was to stall for time. Ned and Trevor would eventually find her. The two security guards and the pathology man would awaken and sound the alarm. Maybe they already had. Then they would follow the trail she had left.

"April told me you used to work in Saint Louis," Nancy said conversationally, keeping her eyes averted from the knife. She couldn't show fear. She couldn't let him know she was buying time. "You knew David Baines and helped get him expelled from medical school."

Rayburn didn't answer. But he didn't continue either.

"Since I'm going to die, do you mind if I make a few guesses as to what really happened?" asked Nancy.

"I don't have much time, Ms. Drew."

"Anna Treadway, a cardiac patient, died because of gross negligence," Nancy said quickly. "The wrong medicine was prescribed. David was to blame, but he wasn't the only one."

Rayburn shook his head vehemently. "It was David's fault, not mine."

"It *was* your fault. You made a mistake. A big mistake. One that would have justified a malpractice suit and maybe even cost you your license. But you blamed it all on David."

"No." Rayburn was clearly agitated. "That's what Shaw thought, but he couldn't prove it."

His admission made Nancy realize she was on the right track. "Maybe not. But Dr. Shaw knew you were to blame. He worked with you at the hospital in Saint Louis." Nancy paused, playing a hunch. "He'd seen you make mistakes before."

"No!"

"It was his recommendation that got you thrown off the staff there. I saw the name on your Boston medical certificate. It was altered to Rayburn. What's your real name? Rayburne?

You took off the last *e* to keep anyone from digging into those years in Saint Louis!"

Rayburn's face turned deep red. "But you won't be around to prove any of this, will you? It's all allegation!"

"Dr. Shaw had proof that you were tossed out of the Saint Louis hospital. That would have opened an investigation into your qualifications. People would have checked more thoroughly into your background."

Rayburn sucked air through his teeth, clutching the surgical knife in a gloved hand. "Shaw was a meddling old fool. He almost recognized me the night he was brought in. I couldn't take the chance he would remember me. I'd been so careful to change my records. Do you think I could have gotten a job anywhere with that black mark against me? As it was, I had to settle for this mediocre hospital, where one cursory background check was enough to convince them I was an excellent doctor!"

"I would hardly call W.U. Med School a mediocre hospital," Nancy said.

Rayburn snorted in disgust. "Well, it's nothing like where I should be. And I didn't kill Anna Treadway! Baines fouled that up all on his own."

"Baines was doing your job for you. He wasn't even qualified to administer medicine. You told him what to do, then let him take the blame." Nancy regarded him seriously. "But you killed Dr. Shaw yourself."

Rayburn closed his eyes, his lips a thin line. For a moment Nancy wondered if she'd pushed him too far. She tugged against the leather bindings and felt one foot slip loose about an inch. Her pulse leapt. If she could just keep him talking a few more minutes!

"I didn't want to kill Shaw," Rayburn admitted, "but I had to."

"How did you do it?"

"I injected air into one of his veins. It caused an air embolism—a bubble. When the bubble reached his heart he had a massive heart attack. It was quick."

Nancy could scarcely believe her ears. If only she had this confession on tape!

Rayburn waved the scalpel, and Nancy said quickly, "David Baines followed you to River Heights."

"That's right. The little blackmailer!" Rayburn spat viciously. "But he'll pay for that."

"He knew who you were and demanded money in return for his silence. That's how he could afford to buy a Porsche." Nancy twisted her left arm, stealing a quick glance at her wristwatch. How long had she been here? Where was Ned?

"There's one thing I'm curious about: why did you pick Trevor to frame?"

Rayburn sighed. "Poetic justice. He was going to be Shaw's son-in-law. I couldn't believe it when April Shaw—*Shaw's daughter*—was accepted to medical school here. I didn't make the connection for a while. She was just another student. And then I overheard her talking to Trevor one day, telling him she wanted to be as great a doctor as her father. I had to check it out."

Nancy could well imagine Rayburn's panic. "You took Trevor under your wing so you could keep track of what was going on with April."

"It was just possible Shaw would never know about me," Rayburn continued. "But then he came to River Heights and became a cardiac patient. *My* department."

"So you planned to kill him. You used some of Trevor's old standard orders, changed the dates, and stuck the new patients' names on them— effectively ordering the wrong medicine and making it appear as if Trevor had blundered. Under the guise of friendship, you ruined Trevor's reputation so that when Dr. Shaw died, everyone would blame Trevor. Even April."

Rayburn didn't deny it.

"Even worse," Nancy added softly, "you endangered other patients' lives."

"Ms. Drew, you don't understand. We're talking about the end of my career. My life! I would never have been able to start over again. Too many people would know."

Nancy didn't remind him again about the lives he'd jeopardized in his selfish pursuit of personal goals. His hands were shaking violently. He was fast losing control. She couldn't afford to antagonize him further.

"You should have taken my earlier warning to heart," Rayburn said sadly.

Nancy cautiously moved her right foot, trying to wiggle it free of its bonds. "You mean the first time you knocked me out with a hypodermic?"

He nodded. "I put you in the stairwell. I was going to push you down, but unfortunately I could hear other people coming. Then, when you and your boyfriend showed up at the anatomy lab, I knew I had no choice. I was going to have to dispose of you one way or another, but first I had to get Shaw's body out of the hospital. I'd been trying to move him for days, but security was everywhere, searching for him."

"How did you move him from the morgue?" Her right foot was free! Keeping eye contact with Rayburn, Nancy worked on the left.

"That was easy. Those morgue employees are as regular as clockwork. I lifted keys from the attendant, made a duplicate, then waited for Shaw's body to arrive. When the attendant went on his break, it was a simple matter to roll the body out of the morgue and through the tunnel. The pathology personnel barely glanced at me."

"What if you'd met someone in the tunnel?"

Rayburn shook his head. "Let's not think about that unpleasant scenario."

"What made you decide to run down David?" Nancy asked.

"That was your fault. You were getting too close. You were pressuring him. The paramedics had just brought some patients into the emergency room. There was a lot of confusion. The ambulance keys were available, so I took them. I was going to follow David, but then *you* stopped him! Don't you see? I had to run him down." He paused, frowning. "I wish he'd been killed outright. I'm going to take care of him as soon as I'm through with you."

"You can't get away with this," Nancy said calmly. "I talked to David. He mentioned your name in connection with Saint Louis. Security's looking for you already."

Rayburn laughed derisively, as if indulging a dull child. "If that were true, those security men wouldn't have been taken by surprise when I anesthetized them. Soon I'll help them search for the mysterious body snatcher I followed through the tunnel. I suppose that's when we'll—uh—learn of your unfortunate demise, Ms. Drew. Now I think we've talked long enough, don't you?"

Smiling regretfully, he tightened his grip on the scalpel, aiming it at Nancy's throat.

Chapter

Seventeen

NANCY STRUGGLED VIOLENTLY, straining at her bonds. Rayburn grabbed her shoulder. The scalpel was poised above her throat. She screamed and bucked. Both feet were free! Swinging her legs, she connected with Rayburn's hand, sending the knife singing through the air. Rayburn howled in surprise. He lunged forward, but Nancy gave him a quick, sharp kick. He spun around.

She jerked her hands furiously, trying to break the leather bindings. Rayburn staggered forward and she kicked out, landing a glancing blow on his left shoulder. His face registered surprise. She twisted her arm, pulling her wrist free, friction burning her skin.

"You can't do this," Rayburn warned.

"Watch me," Nancy muttered through her teeth. She fought to loosen the binding on her other hand, poised to fight off another attack. Rayburn, changing course, turned toward the surgical cart. Out of the corner of her eye Nancy saw him grab another scalpel. With a cry of frustration, she managed to free her other hand, propelling herself off the table at the same time.

Rayburn stuck out his leg, tripping her. Nancy went down and began to crawl frantically forward. He grabbed her leg. She saw the knife slice downward. Twisting, she slammed her foot against his head. The knife hit the floor with a harmless ping.

"You can't—get away—" Rayburn panted.

Nancy was scrambling to her feet, prying his fingers from her leg. Her flailing arm hit the I.V. stand. She pulled it over, slamming it onto Rayburn's back.

Chest heaving, she searched the room for an exit and spotted a pair of swinging doors in the far wall. She ran as fast as she could, slamming against them. Her bones jarred. The doors were locked with dead bolts high out of her reach!

Rayburn's footsteps were right behind her.

Nancy whirled around, her back to the doors, her heart racing.

"I warned you, Ms. Drew," Dr. Rayburn said with a shake of his head. Nancy searched wildly for another avenue of escape.

He stopped a few feet in front of her. "There's no way out," he said, reading her mind.

Think! Nancy willed her brain. Her gaze raked the room. There were weapons galore—every kind of surgical device imaginable. But Rayburn was right; there was no escape.

She crept sideways as he advanced, keeping a small counter between them. The surgical table stood across the room in front of her. Tubes stuck out from the wall and curved snakelike toward the anesthesia machine.

Rayburn stopped, two feet away on the other side of the counter. "I am sorry," he apologized.

"Right," Nancy said. "I can see how sorry you are." She gauged the distance between them. Edging to the right, she watched as he did the same, keeping her trapped behind the counter. He pulled a long rubber tube from his pocket and wound it casually around one hand.

"Strangulation?" Nancy asked, eyeing the tube.

He took a step nearer. Nancy backed up until her heel connected with the wall. Rayburn took a step to the left, watching her closely. Nancy didn't move. He took one more step.

Now! she thought, leaping toward her right. Rayburn lunged forward, his hand narrowly missing her sleeve. Nancy ran to the surgical table. Rayburn's footsteps clattered behind her.

She grabbed the closest anesthetic mask. Rayburn's arm snaked around her waist, yanking her back. Gas was escaping. With all her strength she twisted around, forcing the mask down over Rayburn's face.

He fought like a tiger. His knee connected with the operating table and he stumbled, flailing. Crack! His head hit the floor. He lay dazed.

Nancy strapped the mask to his face, then stepped away from him. She counted the seconds. Fourteen—fifteen—sixteen . . . How long did this anesthetic take to work? Rayburn's head slowly moved back and forth. Twenty-two. Twenty-three—twenty-four . . . Was it seconds or minutes? What kind of anesthetic had she given him? What if it was straight oxygen? She might be helping him more than hindering!

Nancy didn't wait to see. She ran for the door, searching for a stool to stand on.

"Nancy!" a muffled voice called from outside.

"Ned!" she yelled back. "The door's locked. Wait! I'll get it open!"

"Are you all right?" he shouted anxiously.

Nancy spied a small stool and dragged it toward the door. She climbed up on the stool and unlatched the dead bolts. Ned and Trevor stormed in as one. A swarm of security men followed. Seeing them, Nancy slumped against the wall.

"Nancy! Are you all right?" Ned's arms encircled her.

"I am now," she admitted shakily, laying her head on his shoulder.

Trevor was leaning over Rayburn's prone form. "Wow," he said, examining the gas line. "You knocked him out with nitrous oxide. Laughing gas!"

"He knocked himself out. Will he be all right?" Nancy asked anxiously.

"Sure." Trevor chuckled. "We could leave the gas on and give him a nice rest, though. He might be easier to handle."

"Come on," Ned said gently, his arm supporting Nancy's shoulder. "You can tell me all about it on the ride home."

"After we inform the authorities," said Nancy.

"After we inform the authorities," Ned agreed.

"And so that's all there is," Nancy said later that night, seated cross-legged on the Drews' den couch, munching on a sandwich. Ned, Bess,

George, Trevor, and April were in chairs around the room. They all looked at Nancy with wonder.

"I'm so glad you weren't hurt," April murmured, snuggling closer to Trevor. It was clear that the misunderstanding over Suzanne had been resolved. "When Dr. Grafton told me my father had always suspected Dr. Rayburn was to blame for Anna Treadway's death, I got really worried."

"Your father just didn't have proof," Nancy said.

Ned took a bite of his own sandwich, chewing thoughtfully. "When you didn't show up at the emergency room, Trevor and I went down to the pathology lab," he explained. "We found the security men and the lab attendant out cold and the door to the tunnel open. Trevor called for backup, and we started down the tunnel. I saw the piece of coat you left and the name tag, so I knew we were on the right track." He glanced at Nancy's sandwich. "You still owe me a dinner," he remarked teasingly.

Nancy laughed.

Bess's blue eyes were wide circles. "An empty operating room? A crazed doctor? Nancy, it's just like the movie we saw! Creepy!"

"No wimpy heroine, though," George said with a grin.

"He wasn't actually crazed," Nancy corrected.

151

"He just had his priorities confused. He didn't seem to understand the seriousness of his actions. It was Rayburn who took the Deverly file, of course. He was trying to pin all the blame on Trevor, just as he did to David in Saint Louis." Nancy shook her head. "He kept apologizing, hoping I would understand that everything he did was necessary."

Trevor's gray eyes were grateful. "Thanks, Nancy. For everything you've done to help me."

"Help *us*," April corrected.

"How's David?" Nancy asked. "Is he going to be okay?"

Trevor nodded. "He came to while you were fighting it out with Rayburn. He's admitted that he sent you and Ned the fake notes so he could get you out in the parking lot alone. When he grabbed you, he only meant to scare you. Apparently he was afraid you were getting too close to the truth and that you might dry up his blackmail source: Rayburn!" Trevor smiled. "I understand a Detective Ryan is taking his formal statement."

"Detective Ryan!" Nancy laughed. "He'll never forgive me for getting into so much trouble."

"He called to say he's coming by tomorrow," Ned told her. "He wants to hear the whole story from you."

"Well, I'm never going near a hospital again," Bess declared. "It's not safe!"

"Oh, I don't know. I'd trust Trevor and April any day," Nancy said, smiling. "How about you, Ned? Have you decided to go into hospital administration?"

He wrapped his arms around Nancy, squeezing her in a bear hug. "This time I have to agree with Bess. I'll stick to plain old business administration. Working at a hospital is more dangerous than being a detective!"

Nancy threw an arm over her eyes in an exaggerated faint. "But you saved me, you strong, handsome male."

"Wimpy heroine," George groaned.

Everyone broke into laughter.

Nancy's next case:

Owner Marva Phillips asks Nancy Drew to join her at Club High Adventure. High-risk sports are the specialty of the house, but there's been a series of threats against Marva's guests. Someone's playing rough and pushing the club to the edge of disaster.

When Nancy investigates, she discovers that all kinds of games are being played behind Marva's back. Businessman Roger Coleman is determined to buy the club, and Marva's fiancé, Gil Forrest, sees a chance to get rich quick. Suspicious accidents in hang gliding and rock climbing put several guests in peril, but Nancy must play the most dangerous game of all. She has to find out who is trying to sabotage the resort— before the saboteur resorts to murder . . . in *Over the Edge,* Case #36 in the Nancy Drew Files℠.